The Second Bridge

To Ellen.
at the beginning —
Thank you
Gary

2 July '87

Other Fiction by Gary Gildner
The Crush
A Week in South Dakota

The Second Bridge

A Novel
by Gary Gildner

Algonquin Books of Chapel Hill
1987

for Jim Coleman and Paul Zimmer

published by
Algonquin Books of Chapel Hill
Post Office Box 2225, Chapel Hill, North Carolina 27515-2225
in association with **Taylor Publishing Company**
1550 West Mockingbird Lane, Dallas, Texas 75235

Parts of this novel first appeared, in different form, in
Colorado State Review and *Tendril*.

Library of Congress Cataloging-in-Publication Data

Gildner, Gary.
  The second bridge.

  I. Title.
PS3557.I343S4   1987   813'.54   86–17393
ISBN 0–912697–44–X

Part One

I

On the night before Bill Rau's fortieth birthday, his wife is having dinner with a man on their front porch in Iowa. There is candlelight. She is wearing a Russian peasant's black skirt and a simple white blouse open to the beginnings of her breasts. She has prepared Swiss steak with tomatoes. They are sipping red wine. It is late August and a refreshing breeze comes to them through the screens. The round oak table at which they sit, within fingertips, catches the moon's glow. Before the man arrived, before she showered and dusted herself with lilac powder, she polished the table with Old English Red Oil. Were we there, we could smell its sharp odor.

While they are eating, Bill Rau is driving west across upstate New York toward the Blue Water Bridge in Port Huron. His journey, when he arrives at his destination in Michigan, will have taken him thirteen hours. Near Buffalo the CBC was playing a piece by Ravel that he turned off before the final movement. He has eaten a cheese sandwich and an apple. He is saving the pear and peanuts for later. At the end of each hour he smokes a cigarette.

On Friday—three days before—Bill and Jay Rau talked long distance. They talked about her meeting him and their daughter Jenny in Michigan on the following Wednesday. That night she went to dinner with the same man for whom she prepared the Swiss steak on the Monday night Bill was driving toward the Blue Water Bridge. After their dinner, on Friday, they went to Disco City. After Disco City they went to the man's house for a nightcap.

Exactly one weekend before, Jenny caught a twenty-four-inch pike while trolling with her grandfather—Jay's father—on Houghton Lake in northern Michigan. It was the biggest fish she'd ever caught. Her grandfather took a Polaroid picture of her holding up the fish on a leader. She is tanned and smiling in the picture. She is thirteen. She and her grandparents ate the fish that night. In the morning her German shepherd, Missy, secured to a chain, attacked a neighbor's poodle that ran up to it. The next day Missy was taken to the vet's and destroyed.

After crossing the Blue Water Bridge, Bill Rau stopped the car at a gas station and dialed his number at home. It was ten o'clock there. He counted fifteen rings, then hung up. He stretched and tried to touch his toes. In an hour or so he would be at his brother's house in Flint, where he planned to spend the night. He would try to reach Jay again from there. When they talked on Friday, she said she couldn't get away from work in time to fly to Flint for the birthday party on Tuesday. Wednesday night was the soonest she could leave, what with the latest issue to get out.

Jay Rau edits *Midwest Politics,* a quarterly. She and Bill met almost sixteen years ago, in Detroit, where she was a model and part-time student and he was a reporter. She was nineteen, he was twenty-four. They had their first date in October and were married in January, at the church around the corner from the hotel where they often ate lunch. They spent their honeymoon skiing in northern Michigan. That summer Bill resigned from the newspaper and accepted a teaching job at a college in the Upper Peninsula. Jay continued taking classes. They got a dog. When Bill wasn't teaching he worked on the novel he had started in Detroit. Their second year in the U.P. Jenny was born. They found a house in the country, a brick house built on the foundation of a creamery that had been leveled by fire. In the back yard stood a silo, leaning like the Tower of Pisa, and beyond the silo they could see the deep blue of Lake Superior. Across the road was the County Home. Sometimes on autumn nights as they lay in bed listening to the field mice click back and forth overhead, the room would suddenly receive the red revolving light of an ambulance come to take away one of the old. They felt very secure and lucky. Jenny was learning to walk; Bill's novel had been abandoned but his stories were coming along; and Jay found an excitement in her history classes that she couldn't explain. Once, in the middle of a dream, she sat up in bed and announced, "I want to learn no less than everything!" Bill kissed the moonlight on her eyelids.

No one answered when he phoned again from his brother Andy's house. Francie, his sister-in-law, fixed chicken sandwiches. He showed some slides he had taken of the track at Saratoga. He had spent five weeks in upstate New York working on a suite of poems about horse racing. Earlier that summer, Bill and Jay and Jenny had had two weeks together at their cottage on Houghton Lake. When he left for New York, Jenny moved with Missy to her grandparents' place two miles down the lake, and Jay returned to Iowa and the magazine. During their separation they all wrote letters to one another, and Bill and Jay talked on the phone four or five times. Jenny was fishing a lot and learning to water ski. Jay was having the living and dining ·rooms redecorated, and entertaining women friends on the porch.

In a letter dated July 18 she said, "Sunday afternoon I took a break from chores and went by myself to the matinee of 'Coming Home.' Later, sitting in the rubble of the living room, I momentarily felt as though my heart were bombed out. The film moved me—but then I am especially susceptible to one of its themes: good-byes and separations. I am doing well though, happy in my solitude." On July 23 she wrote, "Your letter perked me up so much on this day that began cool then turned heavy with humidity and 95 degrees. I verily hopped upon spying it in the mailbox—and it was next to a letter from Jen, which made my day. Letters from the other two parts of me. I am enclosing Jen's letter—want you to have it too. You kissed me all night long last night."

Their rendezvous was to be at their friends the Callahans' cottage on Lake Michigan on Wednesday, August 23. She was flying in that evening. On July 31 she sent the Callahans a note confirming her arrival time, adding, "Can't wait to see you all again—to see the summer out with you. I would not miss it." She xeroxed her note and sent the copy to Bill, with a postscript: "Love, I just fired this off to Mike and Phyl. What the hell! Whenever I hesitate on a caper like this, I remember what the poet says, 'Life is short and death is long.' I will see you one day after your birthday and give you my present." On August 4 she wrote, "In a dream last night, you and I went at each other monumentally! Today I ached. But I will not dwell on this. Soon I will live it."

The next day, a Saturday, she wrote, "Just now in the mail I received a summons for jury duty. But it is queer in that the time I'm being called for is July 31–August 25. So already one week of that time is gone. Well, I will call them on Monday and find out what I'm supposed to do. If I really am on jury duty through August 25, I won't be able to come to Mich. to meet you and Jen. Darn. But I've always wanted to do jury duty. Am reading E. A. Robinson's 'Merline'—love especially the passages about the Lady Vivian."

Bill wrote back suggesting she ask the judge to excuse her two days early, in order to fetch her daughter home from Michigan. "He'd understand that," Bill said. "Besides, I *miss* you, baby." Then on Friday, August 18, she said on the phone that the clerk's office had messed up: her duty wouldn't begin until September 5. Everything would work out fine for them. She would be at the Muskegon airport at 10:17, as planned.

"Shall we go swimming or something?"

"Or something," she laughed.

"You sound good."

"You do too."

＊

The birthday party on Tuesday was planned for Bill's mother's back yard. That morning Jenny arrived from Houghton Lake, brought down by Schooltz, Jay's father. He told about Jenny's big pike, and she proudly showed the photo of it. Schooltz said he left a busted water pump up north and had to get back to it before Mabel blew a gasket. He gave Bill a box of acorns, tied with a blue ribbon. Bill and Jenny took Val, Andy's daughter, to her music lesson. Jenny went into the practice booth with her. A sales clerk was playing "Honeysuckle

Rose" on an electric piano. "Like to try it?" she asked Bill. He laughed. "All I can play is catch." That afternoon he played tennis with a cousin.

Bill's mother, who is Polish, served golamki, pierogi, ham, roast beef, and fresh vegetables from her garden at the party. Everyone sat under the silver maple her husband had planted and ate until they said they were stuffed. Then Bill's sister, Helen, produced a German chocolate cake. Amy, Louise, Fanny, and Bernie—Helen's four daughters, wearing T-shirts with horses on them—sang Happy Birthday to him in French. One of his presents was a rubber football; a game of touch football was organized. Everyone was sorry Jay couldn't get off work for the party, but understood that those things happen. Bill's uncle Jack promised to catch a nice mess of perch through the ice next winter, and give it to them when they came to Michigan for Christmas. Bill's mother, who has tended to get blue at family gatherings since her husband's death four years ago, was in good spirits throughout. Bill and Jenny stayed that night at her house. He slept in the bed his mother always gave to Jay and him, which was the bed his parents had slept in. On the bureau and walls were wedding photos of her children and school photos of her grandchildren. She and Jenny slept in the room that Andy and Bill used to share, in the twin beds Bill's parents moved to after the children had left home.

Next morning Bill and Jenny drove west across the state. They took the old highway, 21, for a change. They had plenty of time. Jenny, a map of Michigan on her lap, said, "I'll make up something interesting about the towns before we get to them. Especially if they have good names." But they passed through Ovid and Shepardsville, and she said nothing. In St. Johns, the next town, Bill bought ice cream cones.

"You've been fairly quiet."

"Oh, I was just thinking about Grandma and Grandpa's neighbors—how they *all* have little yappers."

"I hear the poodle's owner made a large scene when Missy got it."

"She kept calling it her baby. What happens to older people?"

They drove through Pewamo, Muir, Ionia (a banner announced the "Free Fair"), Saranac, and Lowell. In Lowell a number of large trees were down, their bushy root systems caked dry in the sun; parts of houses and larger buildings lay askew on lawns or pushed into heaps.

"A tornado hit."

Jenny nodded soberly. "We had some warnings up north," she said. "Grandma would start knitting and smoking."

"One struck in Flint when I was a boy."

"It did?"

"I saw blades of grass, in perfect shape, sticking out of telephone poles. The tornado blew them in."

"I don't ever want to get caught in a tornado."

"It struck on the other side of town."

"Good!"

*

When they arrived at the Callahans' Mike was out in the lake, floating on his back. Phyl had just returned from grocery shopping with their three daughters. Everyone got into bathing suits and joined Mike, who produced a small orange rubber duck to welcome them.

Lying on the sand after his swim, Bill heard his daughter say, "This is my thirteenth summer here. And my parents' fifteenth."

"Naturally." It was Sheilah, the Callahans' youngest daughter, who was eleven.

"The summer after I was born we stayed two months! You weren't born yet."

"I know that."

"In my mother's photo album there are all these really corny pictures of us from that summer. I should bring it sometime. You'd die laughing, Sheilah."

"Like at what?"

"Oh, me on a towel—stark naked."

"Gross."

"And my parents and your parents building a sand castle. And your mom cutting my mom's hair and acting strange, you know. And our dads out jumping up and down in the waves. Really goofy."

"I believe it, believe me."

"My dad even took a picture of his and my mom's feet!"

"Very strange."

"Missy's in some pictures too. She was very small, of course."

*

Jay Rau's plane was late. Mike and Phyl fell into a silent movie routine. She was the eye-fluttering, knees-together coquette, he the leering traveling salesman chucking her under the chin with one hand and stroking his Vandyke with the other. A pair of women standing nearby gave him scolding glances. Bill leaned against the Hertz counter and, indicating

Mike, said to the clerk, "That's my uncle Harvey. Think I should put a leash on him?"

"His T-shirt says 'Coach.' It's up to you."

"Heart of gold, that man."

"Waiting for someone?" The clerk slid an emery board across her nails.

"Harvey's intended, over from Milwaukee. For the weekend," Bill whispered.

"Sure."

The P.A. announced Jay's flight. She was among the last to enter the terminal. She wore large gold earrings and a maroon scarf wrapped tight around her head gypsy fashion, and, seeing them right away, smiling, she went quickly toward them. Her lips were a shiny, deep red, her eyes dark. They all hugged and kissed her. She seemed out of breath, as if she had run from the airplane. "You OK?" Bill said. "Yes!" she laughed. Arm in arm they followed Mike and Phyl out to the station wagon.

"Good thing your jury duty dates were changed."

"You!"

"No offense. To prove it, I will commit several illegal acts in your presence, just to give you practice."

At the cottage the four of them stayed up late drinking champagne. Bill reported having been at the rail of the marred Affirmed-Alydar race in which Alydar, though coming in second, was awarded the purse because Affirmed's jock, Pincay, cut in front of Alydar near the clubhouse turn.

"Did you watch it on TV?" he asked Jay.

"With all the wallpapering I forgot to."

"Well, we didn't see any horse races," Mike said, "but we *did* have all of Phyllis' relatives for dinner since we saw you. Many times. It was loads of fun."

"And Michael's been doing his sit-ups. On the sofa bed."

"One of our quality publishing houses rejected my latest collection of poesy. Dispatch arrived by sniveling hunchback two days ago. Trying to be strong about it," Mike said.

"He finally kissed my great-aunt Willie," Phyl said. "They were both drinking Rob Roys out of jelly jars."

"Now I'm gonna write a sex manual, Mother, and amount to something. What's delicious and funky and dripping with intensity these days?"

"I'm just happy to be back," Jay said. "The air smells so *good*."

＊

In the morning Bill and Jay were up before Mike and Phyl and into their bathing suits. Jenny and Sheilah had been up for *hours,* they said, and were having second bowls of cereal. The older Callahan daughters—Sunny and Kate, sixteen and fifteen—were reading science fiction in the living room, where the family's black labrador, Raymond Massey, lay beside the Franklin stove, his nose pointing at an empty champagne bottle on the floor.

Down on the beach Bill and Jay fell into an easy jog on the hard part of the sand. After about two miles they started back, walking. The sun was coming up bright over the pine trees on the bluff.

"You weren't happy with me in July, were you, Billy?"

"What?"

"When Jen got those bites on her arm, and they wouldn't go away, and we had to see the doctor again."

"I did say something dumb, didn't I?"

"You said, 'How many times must we return to crack this case!'"

"That poor nurse. Think she knew I had Polish blood?"

"You said it to her *and* to me. And loud enough for the doctor to hear."

"It's all the damn polyester in the air."

"And then Jen got upset."

"Hey, are you trying to make me feel guilty again?"

"No." She slipped her arm around his waist.

In front of the Callahan cottage they walked out into the lake. The water was cold. They splashed around getting used to it, and then swam out to where the lake changed from green to blue, staying close to each other.

The rest of that day and all of Friday they spent on the beach. Mike and Phyl brought down the canoe and the four of them battled high waves in it, tipping over often. On shore they lay on towels and reminisced about previous summers. Both days Jay stayed in the water long after the others had come in. When Mike teased her about sprouting scales, she replied that *they* hadn't had to sit at a desk the last five weeks. "Allow me to record the face that said that," Bill said. She gave him a model's exaggerated smile and he snapped her picture.

On Friday night under a gauzy moon they stood on the bluff, with their drinks, and listened a long time to the waves lapping below.

"Well," Mike said, "fifteen summers, man and boy."

"I might be selling good used cars now," Bill said, "if I'd got my chance in the big leagues."

"The ways of our people are hard."

"The Sullivans are naming their new baby Oscar," Phyl said. "Lilly sent a note today."

"Do people still have children with the simple tools?" Mike said.

"Oscar Scott Sullivan," said Phyl. "Cheers, everybody." They all drank.

After a while Phyl said, "I don't suppose anyone's interested in a marshmallow roast?"

They all listened to the waves, had another drink, and soon they were sleepy.

*

In the morning Jay said, "Would you mind, Billy, if we left today? I'd like to have Sunday at home, to rest up, before everything starts on Monday. And the house will be a mess—what with the painter and paperhanger."

The Callahans understood; they had to start packing themselves. After a swim and breakfast, good-byes were said and the Raus started off. In the car they talked about getting another dog. Jenny said she'd like either a black lab, like Raymond Massey, or an Irish wolfhound, like Bran, the Sullivans' dog.

"If you get an Irish wolfhound," Bill said, "will you teach it to recite Yeats?"

"Come on, Dad."

"Well now, you've heard Bran recite."

"Sure."

"When you were smaller you believed it."

"When I was smaller I be*lieve* I believed that Bran barked. You and Frank said that stuff about Yeats."

They listened to a Detroit Tigers game until Gary, where the radio started to crackle and fade. "Next summer, Dad, I really hope we can see a game—in Detroit." He told her next summer for sure. "You and Mom *still* haven't shown me the hotel where you ate your famous romantic lunches." After they crossed the Mississippi, which she always waited for, Jenny went to sleep and the sun slipped down in front of the car. "Tell me if you'd like me to drive." "I will." "This is always the longest stretch, isn't it?" "Won't be long now." "I want to get my doctorate, Billy. I'm starting to feel stale."

They arrived home about eight o'clock. The painter and his wife, just finishing up, had spotlights shining on the walls and ceilings of the living and dining rooms. Bill and Jay sat on the porch, out of the glare, and drank a beer. Jenny went to bed.

"Are your ears buzzing?"

"No. But they're all stopped up," Jay said.

"I feel like a zombie."

"I hate that drive."

On Sunday, surrounded by new gold walls, they put the furniture back. Then they took a slow bike ride to Greenwood Park. In the Rose Garden the flowers were brave but beginning to brown and curl. That evening Jay put on a leg of lamb. After dinner they sat on the porch in their rockers. A bright moon shone through their sycamore branches.

"Something's nagging at me," Bill said.

"What is it?"

"That stuff I got in New York really wants to be a novel."

"Oh." She studied her thumbnail, then bit off a piece of skin. "I'm going to start the Ph.D. in the spring."

He was gazing toward the sycamore and didn't seem to hear her. "Have pity on the accused," he said at last.

"What?"

"Your jury duty."

"Yes. Yes, I will," she said.

*

On Monday Bill drove her to her office, then dropped off the leased car and went home to his desk. He answered the correspondence that was waiting, and typed up some notes. On Tuesday he saw his new writing students. On Wednesday he worked on the first paragraph of his novel. On Thursday, after Jenny went to bed, Jay said she had to tell him something.

"I've been seeing someone."

She sat down in the black leather chair across from his desk. He sat on the footstool in front of her.

"He asked me out to lunch, and it just started," she said.

Bill found a cigarette on his desk, but couldn't find a match. He came back, sat on the footstool, and looked at her. She smiled a helpless smile and took his hand.

"When I was gone?" he finally said.

She nodded.

"Are you in love with him?"

"He's very nice to me and . . . I'm very fond of him. What I've decided to do, Billy, is live alone for a while. There are some things I want to think about . . . and I want to become more independent."

"Have you gone to bed with him?"

"Yes."

"And you want to continue seeing him?"

"Yes."

"Of course. Well . . ." He patted her hand.

"I hoped you would understand. Oh, Billy, I hoped that more than anything."

He took a deep breath, smiled, exhaled. "When did it start?"

"About a week after I came back in July."

"And you've been seeing him all along?"

"We met for lunch once a week for the first three weeks. Then we went out to dinner once. And I made dinner for us here once. But you really *do* understand?"

"Yes," he said.

"And you still like me?"

"Look . . . I couldn't stop . . ."

"Oh," she said, "oh just *hold* me."

He took her in his arms.

"Closer!"

They went upstairs to their bed.

Lying beside her afterwards, he looked at the moon shining through the walnut tree outside their windows.

"When will you tell Jenny?"

She put her hand over her eyes and groaned. "Oh my God."

"You knew you'd have to tell her."

"I never thought of it."

He sat up. "You never thought of it?"

"No."

"You said you wanted to live alone."

She nodded.

"To continue seeing this guy."

She groaned again.

"Or were you planning to live with him?"

"He's married," she said weakly.

Bill looked toward the moonlight in the walnut branches. He said, "So you came up here. This bed."

"No. No, we didn't."

"Where, then?"

"At his house. His wife was—" she stopped.

"Not even when you fixed him dinner over here? It would have been . . . convenient."

"I didn't want to."

"Who is this guy?"

"His name is Win." She said Bill had once met him, briefly, at the Steak Pit. She'd known him about four years, she said, but there had been nothing between them until now. He did research from time to time in her building. He was working for a state legislator while finishing his Ph.D.

"Lots of teeth and a mustache," Bill said. "You complained together about your boss—how he was mucking up the magazine or something. I think you also mentioned both having daughters the same age."

"I don't remember."

"Where was his daughter when you were—when you had your romance?"

"I don't know. Staying with her grandparents."

"Where was his wife?"

"Traveling somewhere. Their marriage is a mess."

"That's what he told you?"

She nodded.

"What did you tell him about ours?"

"Nothing."

"What was wrong with our marriage?"

She shook her head. She was crying. "There's nothing wrong with it. There was nothing wrong with it. I love you!"

"Then why? Why do you want to leave us?"

She threw her arms around him. "I don't want to leave you! I didn't mean to say that—it just came out."

He moved away from her. "It just came out?"

"Yes, oh yes! I couldn't hold everything in anymore. My heart was about to burst. Then everything got mixed up."

"I'm starting to feel sick."

"I wanted to *tell* you."

"You told me."

"And you were wonderful, Billy. You were so wonderful and understanding."

"I thought you were in love. You were radiant. I felt . . . helpless. But now—"

"Please take me back."

"I don't understand how you could say you wanted to leave, and twenty minutes later say you didn't mean to say that. Hadn't *thought* about it."

"I didn't think about it."

"Is this a joke, Jay?"

"Oh please believe me."

"Nobody gives up fifteen years without *thinking* about it."

"I think I was temporarily insane."

He slapped her face. Then he got up and walked around the room. His hands were shaking. She was holding her cheeks and sobbing quietly. He sat beside her.

"I'm sorry," he said. "It's very confusing."

"I was terribly lonely and depressed. One night I came home from the office and went to bed at six o'clock."

"Why didn't you tell me when we talked on the phone? We talked four or five times?"

"I don't know."

"You sounded fine. You said so. And in one letter you said you never felt stronger."

"I thought I was being strong. I really did."

"Then I don't understand."

"I didn't say anything because I didn't want to upset you."

"Upset me? Holy Christ, are you afraid of me?"

"I didn't want to disturb your work. I know it's important to you."

"So you take up with some guy and decide to leave us. In order to become more independent. Something stinks, pal. What is it?"

She put her face into a pillow, sobbing harder, and shook her head.

He went downstairs, poured a large bourbon, and sat on the porch. He looked at her bike, its handlebars glossy with moonlight. He said, "I can see you coming home on your bike, Jay, looking fresh and tanned and beautiful. You're wearing white shorts and a T-shirt. You came home every day like that this week. We'd have a beer on the porch. You'd tell about your day, I'd tell about mine. We'd make dinner together. I'd call you Big Momma. You'd call me Big Daddy. Sometimes I'd slap your hind end when you were mixing something, sometimes you'd slap mine. That *is* true, isn't it?"

He poured another whiskey and finished it. Then he went back upstairs. She was lying under a sheet, staring at the ceiling.

"I'm sorry I slapped you."

"I know."

"I've never done that before."

"I know."

He got in bed. The moon was in a corner of the far window.

A tennis ball can stood on the sash, halfway up where the window locked.

"I'm going to call him tomorrow and tell him I don't want to see him anymore."

"Did you see him this week?"

"We had lunch on Monday."

"On Monday?"

She didn't say anything.

"Jay, I'm suddenly thinking about your eagerness for jury duty. I can't help it."

"That isn't true."

"What isn't true?"

"I don't know. Please, Billy, I want to come back. I want things the way they were."

"When you wrote to me about those first dates, you said they'd prevent you from coming to Michigan, to meet me and Jenny. As I remember, you could've served all but a couple of days—it was a matter of getting off two days early."

"Jury duty didn't have anything to do with it."

"With what?"

"With that."

"With your affair."

"It wasn't much of an affair."

"When did it begin?"

"I told you."

"I mean, when did you sleep with him?"

"Please, is that important?"

He said nothing.

"It was . . . just twice."

He said nothing.

"The Friday before I saw you in Michigan."

"You mean the Friday we talked on the phone the last time?"

"Yes."

"Did you know then, while we were talking, what you were going to do? With him?"

"He called me after we talked."

"Then what?"

"He invited me out to dinner."

"Then over to his place?"

"We went dancing first."

"Where?"

She shook her head. "Disco City," she finally said.

"Disco City. That's where my students go to watch the transvestites. Remember when Linda Skyles said we ought to go there? That it was kinky? And how you reacted to the idea? 'Shabby,' I think you said." He got out of bed and stood by the windows. "So you watched the transvestites and then went to his place."

"We went, yes."

"After you and I had talked—that day—about being excited to see each other." He took the tennis ball can off the sash and walked around the room, bending it. "So that was the first time."

"Yes."

"And then you had him over for dinner, the next night, and . . ."

"No."

"When, then?"

"Billy . . ."

He said nothing.

"On Monday."

"The night before my birthday?"

She nodded.

"The night I was driving back to Michigan."

She didn't say anything.

"No wonder I couldn't reach you when I called. That's a wonderful present, Jay. Here"—he tossed the bent can on the bed—"here's something to put our life in."

She covered her face with the sheet. "I was so confused."

"Confused? Are you going to tell me you didn't know what you were doing? That you were drunk and . . ."

She uncovered her face. "Please don't."

"Three lunches—no, four counting this week. Two dinners. One Disco City. And you're ready to give up fifteen years and move out. Even though there's nothing wrong with our marriage, you say, and you love me. What's missing, Jay?"

"Please."

"Please what?"

"I was confused and lonely and depressed."

"I was on my way to *see* you."

"I wanted a baby."

"What?"

"I wanted you to give me a baby," she cried.

"You're lying. We talked about that three or four years ago and both agreed not to."

"You agreed."

"So you decided to get one on your own. With him."

"No."

"Did you wear your diaphragm?"

She didn't answer.

He lay down and stared at the ceiling.

"You've slept with another woman," she said. "I know you have."

"You're lying about wanting a baby."

"Haven't you? That Claire, in New York."

"Yes. But I didn't want to leave you afterwards."

"You're strong, Billy. You don't understand."

"You're right. I don't understand."

"I love you and want you."

"You said you wanted to live alone."

"But I don't! I don't! Don't you want me?"

He said nothing. They lay there in silence and then the alarm went off. She got up. He heard her in the shower and then he fell asleep.

*

Jenny Rau kissed her father awake. "I'm late for school," she said.

"I had a bad dream last night," he said. "Did you hear me walking around and talking?"

"Nope—I slept really hard. Bye."

He showered and dressed and went outside. After standing a moment in front of his house, looking one way, then the other, he began to walk. He walked like someone who had recently had casts removed from his legs, tentatively, gingerly, his hands open at his sides, their palms down; or he walked like someone practicing to be a mime.

Several blocks later he put his hands in his pockets and pulled out an envelope. His name was on it. A note inside said, *I love you. Please help me.* A siren started up, and continued to blow while he stood there. He looked suddenly at the bright blue sky. "Tornado," he said, as if to a companion. He glanced quickly around. Then he read the note again. He closed his eyes and shook his head.

He jogged home and went directly to the telephone. After dialing her office he hopped from one foot to the other, waiting, his eyes closed. A woman answered.

"Is Jay there?"

"She's upstairs right now. Is this Win?"

He put the receiver down. He looked at the gold wall in front of him, at the black leather chair, the footstool. He picked up the footstool and held it, moving it up and down in his arms as if weighing it.

When she came home he was sitting on the porch. He had two beers opened. She sat down across from him.

"I understand," he said.

"Oh, Billy," she said and started out of her chair.

"No, don't move. Stay there. Let's talk. Jenny's upstairs doing her homework." He lit a cigarette. "I've gone over what you told me and I think you're afraid, Jay, to say you're in love with your friend."

"But I'm *not* in love with him. I called him today and said I couldn't see him anymore."

Bill Rau looked at her a moment. "Couldn't see him?"

"Didn't want to."

"What did you say?"

She wet her bottom lip. "I told him that I told you everything," she said slowly, "and that you were angry, and that I—"

"You told him I was angry?"

"Yes . . . and that I wanted to make our marriage work."

"As if it hadn't been working."

"No, I didn't mean it that way."

He got up and walked to the end of the porch. A lilac bush rubbed against the screen. She came and stood beside him.

"Honest, I didn't mean it that way."

"What did he say?"

"He said that's the way it goes . . . and we hung up."

"Those were his words—'That's the way it goes'?"

She nodded.

He took his bike off the porch and rode to Greenwood Park. He rode around the pond, around the Art Center, and then repeated these routes, over and over, until he saw stars in the sky.

When he got home, Jay said she'd made a fresh mushroom soup. Jenny, she said, had eaten and gone to baby-sit. "I told her you were working on something and went riding to think about it."

He pulled off his wet shirt, poured a bourbon, and sat in his rocking chair. Jay got a drink too, and joined him.

At length he said, "What did you talk about?"

"Books," she said.

A woman passed in front of their house, talking to a dog. "Don't pull so hard, Fred," she said. "It's too hot."

"What books?"

"I mentioned one of Joan Didion's essays, and he said he'd read it too."

"Do I know it?"

"It's about California."

"What else?"

"James Joyce."

"A politician's lackey reads—" he stopped.

"He almost has his Ph.D. in history."

"What by Joyce?"

"*Ulysses.*"

"You haven't read *Ulysses.*"

"I tried, once."

"But he has read it?"

"He said it was hard to get into."

The woman with the dog came back. "Heel," she said.

"I also showed him a poem by Adrienne Rich."

"The night you ate here?"

She nodded. "And I showed him your new book."

"From there?" He pointed through the French doors toward the bookcase. "Your copy? The one I wrote in?"

"Yes."

He went in and took a book from the shelf. She was behind him, saying, "No, that's *mine,* that's *mine,*" trying to take it away. He opened it and ripped out a page and handed her the book.

*

The bottle was almost empty. Bill Rau held it, neck toward the moon, and studied the oily surface catching the light. Then he leaned over and carefully set the bottle in the rocking chair where Jay had been sitting. He nodded his head and made gestures with his hand, as if carrying on a conversation. Beyond the lilac bush a man next door appeared on his front porch, and called, "Simon? Simon? Here, kitty." Bill Rau sat back in his rocking chair and pulled his ear.

Jenny came out on the porch. She kissed him good night.

"How did your sit go?"

"Fine. We made popcorn. Night, Dad."

He smoked a cigarette and finished the bottle. Then he set the bottle on the floor and put his face in his palms. "Jay," he whispered, "Jay, Jay . . ."

He got slowly to his feet and went into the kitchen. She lay on the floor, an empty aspirin bottle beside her.

He made her stand up. She looked at him with red, sleepy, watery eyes.

"Did Jenny see this!"

She groaned, shook her head.

"Listen to me," he hissed. "If you kill yourself . . . if you do that to us . . . . I will spit on your God damn grave."

*

On Saturday Bill Rau cut his grass, using an old push mower; a white handkerchief was tied around his forehead; his bare shoulders glistened with sweat. From time to time he stopped, took a long tool from his back pocket, and dug up a thistle. His daughter brought out a basket of clothes and hung them on the line. Afterwards, they sat against one of the walnut trees, drinking lemonade.

"Is your mother up yet?"

"She's in the sewing room, making napkins."

That night Jay went to bed right after dinner. Bill stood for a while in his freshly mowed yard, then came in, and seeing that his loafers were wet from the dew, polished them. He found other shoes around the house, and polished them as well. When he finished, there were nine pairs of shoes lined up on his desk. He hunched down, his eye level with the desk, and sighted along their gleaming toes.

In the morning at breakfast, Jenny said, "Gee, Mom, you

look pretty." Jay wore a green shadow, with flecks of gold in it, around her eyes. She curtsied.

"I know," Jenny said, "let's go horseback riding!"

Bill said that there was work he ought to do.

"Aw, come on, Dad. Not on Sunday."

He called ahead, then they rode their bikes to the stables. It was going to get hot. It was hot already. A man stood with three horses under a large oak, rubbing an ointment around their eyes from a roll-on deodorant bottle. "The flies are beasts today," he said.

"Dad's got Phil again!" Jenny said, patting the horse's muzzle. "And I've got . . . who have I got, Mr. Schott?"

"Bon-Bon, my gentlest one, sweetheart."

"Last time I had Belle. She's gentle too."

"Ah well," he said sadly. "She's gone now. Her time was up. But," he took Jenny by the waist and helped her mount, "Bon-Bon is very, very nice."

"Who have I got?" Jay asked Mr. Schott.

"You, my dear, have the remarkable Prince." He brushed a cluster of flies away from Prince's eyes. "The City wants to pass a new law—things must be slow for the Council—to make us send guides along. But today you are on your own, still." He waved them off. "Have a good time, sweetheart."

They took a trail to the Raccoon River, followed the river upstream a distance, then crossed a wooden bridge to a large meadow bordering Water Works Park. Jenny said Bon-Bon felt like taking her time, and rode last. Jay rode second. Her horse and Bill's, one walking close behind the other, raised a plume of dust that suggested a golden retriever's tail. To their right, the Raccoon curled farther away, brown and flat in the sun.

"Do you hate me, Billy?"

He said nothing. Then he stopped his horse and turned in the saddle, looking back to where Jenny and Bon-Bon had paused under a low-hanging tree; she was picking leaves.

"I hate coming after you like a bloody ferret . . . asking questions that make both of us sick." Then, squinting toward the river, he said, "I want to sell the cottage."

"Why, Billy?"

"I dreamt last night we didn't have it anymore, and a great weight lifted from my gut."

"I feel light-headed suddenly."

He looked at her, surprised. "That's exactly what you said in the dream, Jay."

"I was with you?"

"Yes—we were standing in front of the cottage—which belonged to somebody else now—watching the lake change color. We both felt wonderful relief. We laughed."

"You sound far away, Billy."

"I'm glad you're feeling better."

"You're going to leave me."

He looked at her, squinting; he appeared puzzled. Then he reined Phil off the trail onto the meadow grass, and let him gallop.

*

He was watching Mr. Schott saddle some horses when they came back. Jenny had a forced smile on her face.

"Did Bon-Bon behave?" Mr. Schott asked her.

She nodded, trying to make her smile bigger.

Bill paid him. He and Jenny walked their bikes up the road a ways; they said nothing. He leaned his bike, then hers, against the fence. She hugged him. Beyond the fence, a girl was jumping her horse. She was very pretty in her riding togs and handled the horse well. Bill Rau watched her while Jenny cried into his chest.

"Cry all you want," he said.

At length she wiped her cheeks and caught her breath.

"Mom told me," she said.

He looked back down the road to where Jay stood beside her bike watching them. Then she walked up, slowly. When the three of them stood together, she said, "I told her I became involved with another man, and then told you I wanted to live alone. But I don't want to live alone. I want to live with you and Jen." Some of the gold flecks from her green eye shadow were shining on her cheekbones.

He put his arm around Jenny and they started up the road. A truck came by filled with straw and left a wake of dust. They walked through it. The ditch beside them was rich with Queen Anne's lace and thistles, all under a fine coat of dust. On their right, half a dozen riders about Jenny's age were on a practice course, jumping their horses. Bill and Jenny stopped and leaned against the wood rails that bordered the field where the jumpers were. Bill said he could close his eyes and feel the horses' hooves in the fence. Jenny said she could too. Then she said, "I think she loves us and wants to come back."

"You want her back?"

"If you do."

He looked down the road at Jay still standing where they had left her beside her bike and the field where the girl was jumping her horse, and said he did.

*

When Jay was on jury duty she rode home every day to have lunch with him. They ate on the porch. The evenings were turning cool but the days were bright. Her first case involved a carpenter charged with driving while intoxicated. She said when they retired to deliberate, one of the jurors, a Mr. Hagathorn, stood up and declared, "I think we ought to give this fellow the benefit of the doubt. But if he does it *again*," Mr. Hagathorn shook his finger, "we'll throw the book at him!" Bill went back to the first paragraph of his novel. Tacked above his desk was a photo of the track at Saratoga: a pair of horses, steamy after their morning workouts, came toward him out of the mist rising against the Adirondacks. One day he found among his notes a quote from Kierkegaard, written in her hand: "If a man cannot forget, he will never amount to much." One Saturday morning while they lay in bed watching the rain collect on the windows, she asked if he'd had any good dreams lately. He said no. But there was one, he said, which he'd had more than once. "We were in bed together, feeling good together. I said, 'I wish you could stay the night,' and you said, 'I do too, but I've got to get home.'" She'd dreamt she had made him blind in one eye, she said.

*

In the evenings, after dinner, Bill and Jay Rau took long meandering walks, pushing their feet through the leaves that were beginning to gather in drifts. When they came back they sat on the porch, in their rockers, and drank a bourbon before going to bed. He usually wore a red wool shirt, she a ski sweater. Often they discovered that they were thinking about the same things—like the house they could see Lake Superior from, and the field mice that ran above their heads that autumn. September passed—too swiftly, they said—and then October. When their friends called to invite them out, they made excuses. When they wrote to Schooltz, asking him to put a For

Sale sign in front of the cottage, Mabel replied that they would probably sell their place too and move to Arkansas, where it was warmer. Bill set his novel aside, and returned to poems. The one he finished, which Jenny gave him the idea for, is called "A Short Story About the Octopus"—

> *She lays her eggs and then turns to keeping*
> *a faithful watch over the only babies*
> *she will ever have, protecting and caressing*
> *and blowing water over their unborn shapes,*
> *and all the while she is starving.*
>
> *A scientist wanted to know*
> *why this was so, why the octopus would trade her babies*
> *for certain death. So he captured one and removed*
> *a jewel from between her jellied eyes, and sure enough*
> *as soon as she oozed out the last egg she abandoned*
> *her faithful heart and began to feed.*
>
> *What did science discover?*
>   *That lengthening life*
> *is possible by putting out the body's best light?*
> *That one is not fully alive unless she is writhing*
> *and sucking along the ocean floor, her mouth suffering*
> *for mussels and snails?*
>
>   *My daughter*
> *brought this story home from school one day, the day I*
>   *wanted*
> *to be in love with you, who are nothing like an octopus,*
> *though you are starving all the time,*
> *as I am, and would change nothing.*

2

The weekend before Thanksgiving, Schooltz and Mabel came to Des Moines for a visit. They brought clothes, books, skis, brandy glasses, and other things from the Raus' Michigan cottage (Mabel had sold it for them), plus a bushel of cooking apples from Mabel's brother's orchard in Illinois. Bill helped Schooltz unload his pickup, then fixed stiff martinis all around. Jay asked after the Illinois relatives and Mabel, half through her drink, said they were all dying. "Old age is a filthy, filthy trick," she pronounced. Schooltz, trying for a better mood, said everyone was fine, just weathering a little . . . except Uncle Clarence who broke his elbow. "He was painting and fell off the ladder."

"Well now he didn't either," Mabel said.

"What?" Schooltz said.

"He fell off the awning."

"The awning?" Schooltz laughed.

"He was standing on the awning and fell."

"Awning wouldn't hold him."

"That's why he fell," Mabel said.

"Clarence weighs two hundred pounds. Why would a man that heavy stand on an awning?" Schooltz said.

"To paint the trim."

"Have it your way. His elbow's still broke."

"Reva told me he was *standing* on the awning."

"That's right."

"She's his wife. She ought to know."

"That's right."

"So that's how it happened," Mabel said, and lit a cigarette. "And since everyone is avoiding the subject," she added, "I just want to say that selling that lovely cottage was a big mistake and a shame." She also wanted another drink.

Early the next morning, Saturday, Jay and her father were in the kitchen peeling apples side by side at the sink, talking quietly, when Bill came in for a glass of milk. They stopped talking. After several moments Schooltz said, as if the silence were weighing them down and everyone needed a lift, "By golly, she's put me to work, Bill. We're building you a pie!" Bill patted them on the backs, said good, he'd like that, then got his tennis racquet and went off to the courts. When he returned Schooltz met him in the front yard, looking puzzled. "How was your . . . ?" he flagged his three-fingered hand at Bill's racquet.

"I just hit against the board. It's too cold—"

"Listen," Schooltz said and took his son-in-law's arm, walking him away from the house. They stopped beside the big sycamore. Chipping off bark with his thumbnail Schooltz said, "Jay told me . . . I mean about that stuff that happened." His gray eyes were watery.

"What stuff that happened?"

"This summer," Schooltz said, looking old and tired.

The two men stood there facing the sycamore as if they had an appointment with it, as if they had come to it for advice or a reprimand, hanging their heads. Finally Bill Rau walked away.

He stayed in the shower a long time. When he got out he remembered something and was careful drying himself. A few days earlier, after a shower, he'd noticed blood on his legs. He wiped it off but could find no break in the skin. Then he saw blood on his ankles. He wiped it away and again found no wound. Looking down he saw that the white towel he stood on had several drops of blood on it, between his feet. He cupped his testicles. When he brought his hand up his palm was bloody. He found the wound, a clean puncture, and thought of Memory's long fingernails.

Downstairs Jay was drinking coffee at the dining room table. Her apple pie occupied its center on a doily; an odor of cinnamon and cloves was in the air. She told Bill that Schooltz and Mabel had taken Jenny shopping; they wanted to buy her something. "Then they're leaving for Arkansas . . . to look over some property. They're sorry they'll miss Thanksgiving with us."

"Why did you tell that poor old bastard?" When she didn't seem to hear him he repeated the question, over and over, his hands gripping the table and violently rocking it in a rhythm to his question. Jay grabbed her pie and backed away, watching Bill rock the table until it collapsed.

Bill Rau carried the broken table down to the basement and put it by the drain where the rat had slipped out. He stood beside the gleaming mahogany wreckage and saw his figure reflected there . . . and then imagined finishing the job properly with his axe, not in anger but with a dull sweaty determination to produce a tidy pile of kindling and then putting a match to it.

*

36

Dried figs from Greece, fried grasshoppers from Japan, fillets of anchovies from Portugal, wild rice (Extra Fancy) from Ontario, kiwi fruit, sardines, crabmeat—these were among the things which slipped easily into his parka pocket and which on his morning walk to the supermarket he stole.

Usually he got to the store just as it opened. The butchers, the produce manager, the ladies behind the deli cases were still waking up, while he, having already walked a brisk mile, was fresh, alert, and wanting to do something with his hands. A few mornings, though, he was early. He waited outside the door with the regulars who got their breakfast in the store's coffee shop—the man who wore bright red or green trousers and complained about the high cost of flying to Florida; the tiny black woman who always said, "Mercy me, it's a chilly dog"; the cab driver who wore tap-dancing shoes; the heavy woman who smoked and coughed and clicked her false teeth; the old man with the patch over his eye who greeted Bright Trousers either as "Mr. Slim" or "Charlie, me boy" and received a cold stare in return; and Beets, an economics professor from Bill's college who sang in local amateur musicals and whose wife had recently left him. The first couple of mornings that Bill waited outside the door, Beets pretended not to see him (they knew each other to say hello); after that Beets stayed in his car until the store opened. A friend of Bill's in the English department, who played poker with Beets, said that Beets one time ate a cigarette, filter and all, after winning a big pot. Waiting for the store to open, Bill Rau recalled that anecdote and wondered who might be crazier—Beets or himself?

One morning after he'd taken a packet of figs he heard the manager being called on the store's paging system. "George, up front, please. Up front, George." It sounded urgent. Bill was pushing his cart toward the meat section at the rear of the store; at the end of the aisle he saw three clerks gather together behind their dollies and look in his direction. The figs in his pocket seemed suddenly a great weight and the back of his neck got warm. He turned around and headed for the front of the store, where he planned to turn again and go down another aisle and dump the figs. At the front, however, the manager, red-faced, was running straight at him. Bill froze. His heart beat once. But the manager ran past him and out the door, followed by one of the butchers. They returned, struggling with an attractive woman in a camel-colored coat. She cried something, and the manager snapped, "You should've thought of that before!" Bill Rau felt hot all over. "Hold her," the manager told the butcher. The butcher held her; he also held a piece of beef wrapped in cellophane.

"Let *go* of me. Let *go*," the woman pleaded, throwing back her head, her eyes like a pony's.

The manager, dialing his phone, said, "I've got her purse, Milt. She won't run. Let her go." They all three were breathing hard, but the stout butcher was breathing hardest. He released her arm. She glanced over at the check-out women—who looked quickly down, avoiding her wild eyes—then she broke for the door.

"Never mind, Milt. The police'll find her, damn her sticky fingers."

Bill Rau's check-out woman looked sullen, and her bagger pulled at his chin. "She left her little kid," the bagger said. "It's still in the store somewhere."

"But she didn't get the meat," the checker said with grim

satisfaction. "They been costing us a *lot* of money. About time we got that one, kid or no kid." She said to Bill, "Seven on the nose." Her eyes seemed made of stone.

When Bill arrived home he was sweating. But the incident did not cure him; if anything it provided a sharper sense of risk, which was alternately attractive and shameful to him. He also continued to think about the woman: in his fantasies she no longer ran wild-eyed away from the store, but toward him, her camel-colored coat open, her hands like luna moths. And the child was not hers, but theirs.

Then he met Memory Mitchell. She was twenty-seven and worked for an insurance company. She was standing beside her white Corvette one morning, tapping her foot and breathing hard, staring at a flat tire. Bill came along and changed it for her.

That Corvette, Bill soon learned, meant a great deal to Memory Mitchell, and she did not mind at all telling him, in detail, how she got it. She'd been married to a man in computers. "He was making big money but *I* couldn't have my own wheels!" He'd drop her off at the insurance company on his way to work, pick her up on his way home. "I hated every inch of that," she said. One day she announced that if she couldn't have a car, she wanted a set of drums. "He said he'd take me to go buy them as soon as he cleaned his spark plugs. But I knew he'd just try to talk me out of it—say it was a waste of money or I'd disturb the priests—hah!—so I said no thanks, I'll take the damn bus."

"Priests?" Bill said.

"We lived behind the rectory. Fred went to school with one of them. The butterball one."

She rode downtown on the bus and bought what she wanted—the Cozy Cole model. On the ride home, holding the sticks and brushes in her lap (the music store would deliver the drums and cymbals), she sat across from a fat woman who had a dirty baby on one side of her and a basket of dirty laundry on the other. Running up and down the aisle, putting his hand on the passengers and saying what number they were, was a dirty boy.

"Quit that, Cecil!" the woman snapped. "Quit it!"

But the boy continued to run up and down. The woman rolled her eyes as if to say, "What can *I* do?" She noticed a black scab on her elbow and started to pick it. When the scab bled, the woman caught a dollop of blood on her finger, examined it, then thrust the finger in her mouth. Memory shut her eyes and imagined she was home playing her new snare.

"You lebbenteen," the dirty boy said, touching her bare arm. "You lebbenteen," he repeated, planting himself squarely before her, his two big toes on the edges of her sandals.

"All right," Memory agreed, moving her feet away.

"You lebben*teen*!" the boy shot back, showing a pair of large yellow buckteeth.

Memory wished to hell the mother would show some smarts by calling her kid off, but she continued to pick at her damn elbow.

"You lebben*teen*!" the boy cried again. "You lebben*teen*! You lebben*teen*!" Tears were falling down his cheeks.

Memory called to the woman—louder than she meant to, and in a tone that reminded her of her own mother, "Madam, your little boy is unhappy."

The woman regarded Memory coolly, and said, "He ain't

mine, lady, oh no. This'n here's mine," she pointed to the baby, "but not him, no sir. An' I ain't no madam, neither." Then she let out a laugh that filled the bus, and reaching across the aisle she cuffed the boy hard on the head.

"Well, that really got the kid fired up," Memory told Bill. "He kept bawling I was lebben*teen,* lebben*teen,* lebben*teen* until I just could not take it anymore. I got off the first chance I had and ran home. Lost my brushes, broke a sandal strap, and decided to leave Fred. I packed up on the spot. He said, 'If you walk out that door I am keeping the house and all the money!' Hah! I laughed to myself. I got a good lawyer and Fred got exactly half. Plus"—she jingled the keys to the Corvette—"I got the baby that goes with these," and she gave them a smack with her lips. "You want to split another R.C. Cola?"

*

At least three times a week Bill Rau chopped wood in the back yard. The manx was living in his garage then. He would suddenly appear just outside the door that wouldn't close tight (it was warped), his short stocky forelegs planted firmly among scattered wood chips, his rump high, his eyes looking straight into Bill's. Sometimes Bill kept the manx's stare while bringing the axe down hard, but the animal never blinked. After a slow survey around, he'd saunter past Bill across the yard, his shoulders working their muscles loose and his head not once turning around, no matter how much noise Bill made.

Likely the manx picked the Raus' garage because they didn't use it much (they didn't own a car) and because of Ninner, the little white female who lived in the house directly behind theirs, with the Lithuanian woman. Jenny named the manx Mr. Ninner, and soon everyone in the neighborhood was calling him that. But a name meant nothing to him. Nothing seemed to matter to him except Ninner who, when they were seen together, followed him like a squaw her brave, walking several lengths behind. The Lithuanian woman took a fancy to the manx and tried several times to entice him up to her door, holding out a dish of something to eat. But he would not even recognize her. He simply stood beside the raspberry bushes, which divided her yard from the Raus', and waited for Ninner.

One night, opening a window in her basement apartment, Memory Mitchell saw the manx looking in at her and vowed to win him over. She began leaving tins of tuna beside the window. Bill Rau told her, "He gets all the rabbits and mice and squirrels he wants in my back yard. That tuna won't do it."

"Hah! I understand male cats," she said, "and they understand me. I wouldn't touch a female, not fixed or costing a thousand bucks. But I'll get *him*. You want to know the names of all my cats?"

"Sure."

"I'll name them in order. Buster, Boots, Elvis, Andrew MacAndrew, Wally B. Good, Leonardo, Muscles, White Sox, and Sows. Sows is for Son of White Sox, in case you're wondering."

"I was wondering about all of them."

"There's a connection between their names and what I was interested in during that particular point in my life. Leonardo, for instance, comes from when I had a crush on a painter. You could write a book about me."

"That tuna will attract rats," Bill Rau said.

"Hah! Not with that big guy around. You interested in writing a book about me?"

"No. What happened to all your cats?"

She shrugged. "One thing or another. Gave them away, mostly." She looked at him sidelong. "You want to know when I lost my virginity?"

"Not especially."

"I was twenty! Fred got it. And I never slept with *any*body while we were married. You believe that?"

"Why not?"

"Hah!"

"Listen, you don't have to tell me these things."

"Could be I'm lying."

"How many cats have you had?"

"Nine!" And she named them again, fast, as if the nine names were one. Or a hip brokerage house. "Thought you'd catch me."

Bill Rau laughed.

"What's so funny?"

"Me."

"*You!*"

"Yeah, me. I'm a riot."

＊

The woman at the dry cleaner's handed Bill Rau a note he'd written that she found in the pocket of his red wool shirt. It said: "Eyes open. Rises and stretches. Licks hands; washes face; washes behind ears, continuing to lick hands at intervals. Licks fur of flanks, stomach, back. Licks toes, licks, scratches, licks, scratches. Scratches flanks and belly from front to back. Licks genitalia. Licks tail, holding it in hands. Licks hind legs. Bites fur."

One morning in October after Jay had left for work, Jenny

and her father came into the kitchen and discovered a new loaf of bread half eaten, the exposed end a concave wound. The bread had been on top of the refrigerator, a slippery climb. Up till then, Bill thought they were dealing with a field mouse or two wanting a warm place out of the autumn chill to snack and dance, and he'd set a couple of Havaharts. But this was a big bite.

"They're very smart, aren't they, Dad?"

"Strong leapers too. Shall I cut off this part and make us some toast with the rest? Hate to waste it."

"I don't think I want any."

"Suppose they touched it all over?"

She nodded, making a face.

"Probably did," he agreed. "To get a good grip."

Jenny ate a bowl of Cheerios and rushed off to school. Bill cut off the chewed-on end and took it outside for the birds. He studied the salvage. No paw marks that he could see. What the hell, he thought, and cut two slices, toasted them, and, spreading on lots of butter, said, "Nothing like toasted home-made bread. No sir." He was about to bite in when he saw a long black hair on the butter knife.

He called Casey Macey, "The Critter Ridder." The woman who answered said, "He's on maneuvers." Bill left his number. Minutes later the exterminator called him back, from his truck. "This is truck control one. Truck control one. Do you read me?"

"I've got a rat," Bill Rau said, "and it's after my wife's potato-wheatgerm bread."

Ten minutes later Casey Macey, slender and pale with shoulder-length red hair, was in the Raus' kitchen, opening cupboards, pulling out drawers, shining his flashlight. In the back of the silverware drawer a turd lay curled in the fancy sugar spoon they never used.

"Let's investigate the dirt," Casey Macey said.

They went downstairs. The exterminator slipped through the small door that led to the crawlspace under the front porch, looked around, came out. "Negative," he said. "Where's more dirt?"

The house's previous owner had made an addition to the kitchen. The crawlspace under it was got to through a hole in the wall behind the furnace. Casey Macey went in, quick and spidery, and found the burrow.

"Want to see it?"

"I'll take your word," Bill Rau said.

"You got daylight in here. A crack in the foundation—just big enough for it to've squinched through. Likely a female." The exterminator came back to the hole in the wall, and held up a ragged pigeon wing. "If you're shooting these, don't leave the corpses around."

"I'm not shooting them."

"They favor apples an awful lot too."

"Why a female?"

"They like a nice place to have their babies in, like females anywhere." Casey Macey dropped down from the hole, produced a comb, and swept cobwebs and dead flies from his hair.

"Let's git her quick," he said. "From them droppings I'd say she ain't had her litter yet. We'll come back this afternoon with gas. Stick the hose in the burrow, squirt, squirt, and when she comes out, bam! I use a putter myself. Partner likes a wedge. Those things," he shined his flashlight on the Havahart beside the furnace, "are generally worthless."

An image of two men clubbing a rat to death in his basement came to Bill Rau, and he said, "Can't you trap the damn thing?"

Casey Macey raised his eyebrows. "There's glueboards," he said.

"What's a glueboard?"

"Piece of cardboard with a lot of goo on it. Put a little tuna in the center. Rat comes along, sniff, sniff, and gets stuck for lunch. They're kinda fun too. But cyanide's the beauty."

Casey Macey returned with his partner and the gas. They squirted, had their golf clubs ready, but no rat. "She's either down there dead or too smart for us." In case she was too smart, Casey Macey laid glueboards around the basement. Bill Rau troweled cement over the crack in his foundation.

A few days later Jenny went down to use the washing machine and screamed. Bill ran to her. Trembling, she pointed at the sewer drain—the iron grate was pushed aside. "I saw it! I saw it! It was *this* big!" Bill found some bricks to set on the grate. A week or so later he fixed Memory's flat tire, and a week after that he broke the dining room table. On Christmas night he remembered one of the glueboards—the one that sat on the edge of the hole leading into the crawlspace under the kitchen, the glueboard whose caramel-colored goo oozed over the side to hang down in slowly lengthening skinny strings, collecting dust, some of the strings almost four feet long, undisturbed by rat or human hand—on Christmas night he remembered that glueboard and saw it alive with squealing rats biting each other and themselves to get free.

*

The week before Christmas Jay brought home a tree and she and Jenny got out the lights and balls to decorate it. It was the Raus' first cut tree—their first Christmas in Iowa—in seven years. The last three Decembers they were at the cottage, where they strung popcorn and cranberries on the Norway pine in the front yard; and before that they were in Spain, California, and Florida at Christmas. Untangling a nest of colored lights, Jay said, "It's not so bad being home, is it?" Jenny announced that she was extremely happy they were home. "I just want to be *normal* for a change," she said.

"We were normal enough in Spain," Bill said. "On Christmas morning we sat on the beach and watched some fisherman haul in a fairly good net of sardines. Later, you and I played Ping-Pong wearing floppy sombreros."

"You call that normal?"

"You giggled a lot."

"They also had squid, an octopus, and a big stingray in the net," Jay said.

"They threw that ugly sting ray back," Jenny said.

"And Christmas Eve we all ate at La Piscina," Jay said.

"Remember the singers?" Bill said.

"Yes! I loved that old man who was directing them."

"But I know what Jenny means," Bill said. "He should've had a big white muff pasted on his mug. And a red suit and gummy eyes."

"Very humorous," Jenny said.

"I'd like to go back," Jay said.

"Would you?"

"Yes! Why can't we?"

Bill looked at her. He said, "We could go back. We really could, Jay."

Jenny said, "You guys are floating, you know that?"

"Oh honey," her mother said, twirling around with foil icicles flying from her outstretched hands, "what's wrong with floating!"

"Everything! I mean, nothing if that's what *you* want to do. But I want to swim!"

Bill laughed. "Meantime, ladies, your tree's going to tip over." He knelt beside it. "Take those balls off. I'll saw the bottom even and we'll start from scratch."

"Thought you didn't want any part of this," Jay said, dropping, one at a time, foil icicles on his head.

"My old man couldn't brook shoddy construction either."

*

Bill Rau's father got only as far as the third grade in his formal education, so when he appeared to him in a dream that night, quoting from Emerson's "Nature," Bill was surprised.

"That's pretty advanced stuff, Dad."

"Don't forget," he replied, "I went to a country school, and had to hike a couple of miles over cowpies to get there." Giving Bill a big toothy smile, he continued with Emerson: "'Of that ineffable essence which we call Spirit, he that thinks most, will say least. It is this which gives that piquancy to the conversation of a strong-natured farmer or backwoodsman, which all men relish.'"

Bill was about to ask if, as a carpenter, he didn't feel funny saying words like "ineffable" and "piquancy"—but his father was now winding up to fire a baseball at him. Bill was very happy to see him again, to be playing catch under the trees they'd planted. Suddenly his father stopped and held up a finger. "Speaking of shoddy construction, please do not include the thistle, heal-all, cattail, milkweed, loosestrife, motherwort, dock, and black-eyed Susan."

"I won't, Dad. Honest to God I won't."

"'Give me health and a day, and I will make the pomp of emperors ridiculous.'" He doffed a lopsided stovepipe hat and walked away.

Jay nudged Bill awake. ". . . you were laughing," she said.

"I had a funny dream." He told it to her. Then she said she had a dream too, only it wasn't funny. She was in church, she said, and a young boy, about fourteen, was celebrating Mass in street clothes. At the Communion two men needing a shave held up a black sheet, preventing the congregation from stepping forward . . .

Jay wasn't Catholic, but one Sunday in the fall of their second year in the Upper Peninsula, when she was three months pregnant, they went to Mass at St. Peter's Cathedral. As the last notes of the choir's last hymn settled among the statues and votive candles, among the echoes of the Monsignor's Latin, she whispered to Bill, blushing, "It's so . . . *grand!*" That week she found a priest to give her instructions. His name was William O'Donnel, and they hit it off beautifully. Not only did they share an enthusiasm for the poetry of the Roman Church, but they had a deep common interest, it developed, in nineteenth-century Europe as well. Telling Bill about her meetings with the priest, about their discussions of the mysteries of the Virgin Birth and Transubstantiation, about the growth of Liberalism, the rise of Nationalism, the Revolution of 1848, about Mazzini, Garibaldi, Kossuth, Bismarck, Napoleon the Third—

telling Bill about all that richness she would suddenly cup her hot cheeks and sigh, as if to continue would set her on fire.

She blushed easily and deeply and the snow fell, Bill remembered. On New Year's Eve they danced in the ballroom of the Northland Hotel, her belly large and beginning to move from within, and she whispered, "Here, oh put your hand *here,*" helping him find the kicking place. Her face shone brilliantly. Walking home on the deserted icy streets, holding each other, Jay took his hand and again placed it on her belly. "There . . . there," she murmured as if calming her heart. Then Jenny arrived and the blush in her cheek was alive as ever, no matter what the subject matter was—nursing, baptism, or the unification of Italy. And Father O'Donnel—who blushed a lot himself—fit right in. When he came for tea he stuttered and searched for a better word or a lost date with amused frustration, and twice he went away without his hat. They were all four involved, Bill felt, in a giddy ceremony whose name, when he tried to think of one, was never good enough. Just before Jenny was born Bill and Jay took long walks in the woods behind a farm they admired, though it wasn't much of a farm anymore, and from a hill about a mile away one of them would turn and point to its leaning silo, as if seeing it for the first time:

"*That's* where we should live."

"In a real castle!"

"Or in a lighthouse!"

"We'll raise goats!"

William O'Donnel baptized Jenny in St. Peter's on a crisp spring morning. Bill could smell wine at the font. O'Donnel looked pale and tired, but Jenny, dressed in a long lace gown with a frilly hood attached, had the color of wild strawberries in her cheeks. And her eyes glittered. St. Peter's sat high above the town; from its main portal, after they all stepped out with Jenny wrapped snug in Jay's arms, they could see two figures on a large floe broken off from the lake's main crust, waving their arms, and in closer, three men pushing a boat toward them. They all stood where they were until the two figures were saved. Then O'Donnel excused himself from the luncheon party and hurried back inside the church.

Early that summer he left Marquette. A note to Jay apologized for his sudden departure: he said he required a climate less severe. He recommended someone to continue her instructions. He left no forwarding address. When Jay inquired at the Monsignor's office, his secretary was evasive, saying only that Father O'Donnel was a private man whose health was not good. She called on the priest whom O'Donnel recommended, but she did not see him a second time. That was the end of her instructions.

Now in Des Moines, Bill and Jay lay side by side, on their backs, waiting for the morning light. He thought about how often in the past weeks they had been wakened by dreams, telling them to each other, then staying awake, their hands sometimes touching, until dawn. They seemed to be waiting for something. For what? Field mice to suddenly scamper in the rafters? Lake Superior to appear beyond their back yard, so they could get out of bed and go down and jump in and squeal with delight?

A melancholy thought occurred to him: that their life in the Upper Peninsula was only a story now. The house with the leaning silo, the dancing mice, O'Donnel—these were all inventions—and as inventions they could be altered, worried over, *improved*. O'Donnel was a drunk. Who probably left town because he was in love with Jay and could not declare it. Make him sober now, composed among his books. Only a story, their life. A comic strip. Bill could see it—the characters were stick-figure drawings by a child, their eyes big round empty circles. The balloon above one character's head said: "Shoplifting, Memory Mitchell." Bill Rau inhaled deeply. He felt stupid.

Jay said, "Let's sell the house and go back to Spain, Billy."

They were floating, Jenny said. Bill Rau imagined a great expanse of water. He was on his back in it. Well, this is nice, he thought. Then he saw the beach at Nerja, an octopus writhing under a net, hundreds of sardines flipping silver and gray all over it as if the octopus were afflicted with a kind of terrible dancing hives. He saw himself out in a boat at the cottage, pulling in a northern pike he'd hooked in the flank; it was angry as hell, slapping against the gunnel. He saw a powerful speed-boat throwing up a roostertail, racing away.

"We can do it," Jay said.

He saw them in Detroit that October they met, boarding a sailboat, and taking it up the Detroit River to Lake St. Clair, to the channel above Drummond Island, their sails at full blos-som. Through the channel and across Lake George they sailed, to the locks at Sault Ste. Marie. They sat on deck in one of the locks while the lock filled and raised them to the higher level of Lake Superior. Then they sailed across the big lake, Jay man-ning the jib all the way, her cheeks aflame, to Marquette, where they picked up Jenny who waved to them from the end of an ore dock. They tacked then and returned to the locks, down

Lake Huron, under the Blue Water Bridge, past Detroit to Lake Erie ("Any fish in this green sludge hole?" he called to a fisherman. "No, just one old retired turtle, devoted to brooding"), up Niagara Falls to Lake Ontario, and then out the St. Lawrence Seaway to the Atlantic and the Hotel Atlantico in Cadiz, Spain, just the three of them.

Devoted to brooding? Bill heard the pigeons waking up under the gables, starting and starting their engines. It was a sound, especially when he was trying to work, that he sometimes went out and threw stones at. They'd had pigeons twelve years, enough was enough, the roof was going to hell. The previous spring, he remembered, a pigeon lived in the gutter below their bathroom windows. Every morning she made her engine-starting purr while they brushed their teeth. Bill would tap on the glass and tell her that as soon as she had her chicks she had to clear out. That Halloween eye of hers just stared. Early one morning when they were still in bed, they heard something heavy fall on the roof in a loud *whoosh,* followed by a harsh scraping sound. They went outside and saw that several feet of stucco had fallen off the fireplace chimney and cascaded directly over the pigeon's nest. Bill went up a ladder. She was trapped in rubble, rapidly blinking that orange and black eye at him. He dug her free and carried her down.

"Can't we save her, Billy?"

"Look at her."

He took the pigeon out to the woodpile where his axe was. Then he put her and the dead chicks in a garbage sack.

Now, as the new pigeons purred, he saw himself taking a rake up on the roof to claw out their nests. Rake Man, Professional Pigeon Killer, No Bird Too Small! He'd arrive at his jobs in a horse-drawn covered wagon, a lopsided stovepipe hat on his head.

"Don't you want to talk about it?" Jay said.

"I'm sorry, pal. I was off being stupid."

"Last night you sounded excited about Spain."

"I was excited."

"If I quit my job before June, I can collect all the money that they've taken out for retirement. It's five or six thousand dollars. Add that to everything else and we're practically rich!"

"We had a good time there."

"Oh we did. And this time we'd get our own house."

"What about Jenny?"

"She'd love it, you know she would. We'd find a nice school for her and—"

"She wants to swim, you know."

"Billy, we'd *all* swim."

In circles? he thought. Just then the alarm went off.

※

It was bitterly cold the next few days, their boots squeaked in the snow when they walked, but the Christmas tree was up and sat level, the seven-year-old lights made in Taiwan still worked, and Jay offered to give Jenny a permanent that would look like her favorite singer's. She said she'd think about it.

One evening when Jenny was at her friend Sophie's, Bill and Jay wrapped presents and talked again about selling the house, quitting their jobs, and moving to Spain. They were drinking bourbon and had a nice fire going, and by the time the wrapping was finished they'd made up their minds. What *was* stopping them! Bill put an album of Strauss waltzes on the stereo and they danced around the room, Jay's cheeks flushed, the tree lit up, the fire blazing, its flames reflected in the French doors, the clean odor of pine mixing with everything, and yes, they said, yes! They would find a villa in the mountains, in little Ojen, where they bought fish and fruit and watched moonlight lie on the sea far away.

"A villa was for sale there, remember?" Jay said.

"Yes, and you wanted to buy it."

"I was thinking ahead!"

Round and round they went, from Ojen to old Vienna, where Johann Strauss the Younger kept time with his fiddle bow. "My name—excuse me, Fräulein—is Yosef!" "And you haf such big eyes!" Then Jenny came home and they pulled her into the dance, the three of them laughing, stepping on each other's feet, and Bill said, "Remember the New Year's Eve when we danced with Jenny still in your belly?" Jenny said, "Pull-eze, Dad, don't get mooshy." "Mushy?" "*Moo*shy *moo*shy *moo*shy!" Jay slipped out, letting father and daughter have a waltz to themselves, lifting her glass to them, her moist eyes catching the flickering light from the fire. Bill and Jenny danced in a circle around Jay, going round and round, their elbows rising and falling in foolish exaggeration to the waltz's rhythm, and then as Johann Strauss the Younger brought "Delirien" to a big finish, sending a thousand dancers into their final swirls, Bill and his daughter, their arms making a lasso, captured Jay, who closed her eyes in their embrace. They stood like this until the violins died, the arm returned to its slot, and the record stopped with a snappy click.

＊

The next day Bill called Memory at her office. He wanted to see her.

"Not tonight," she said. "Thursdays I meet with my discussion group. By the way, one of your students is in it. How about the first day of winter?"

"When's that?"

"Friday. Can you wait?"

"Yes."

"Hah! I'll have a surprise for you!"

So after dinner on Friday, Bill Rau went out to stop things with Memory Mitchell. And no more shoplifting! He'd mail the store some money and praise the friendliness of its staff.

All the houses on Memory's street sat on a high bank—two- and three-story houses that were, many of them, divided into apartments and rented out to students and young singles. Next door to Memory's, two black kids were sliding down the icy bank on a piece of cardboard. They were bundled up to their eyes and squealing and Bill remembered a hill in Flint that he used to go down when he was their age, a *long* hill, Lyle's Hill, at the bottom of which was Miller's Pond, and man, when he hit that pond his sled was flying!

One time, his buddy Freddy Zielinski and he were going down on Freddy's Airline Pilot, and the run was hard and slick from about a week's use and a good freeze, and a mouse appeared at the edge of the pond, directly in their path, and sat up and looked at them! They hit the mouse with a runner, practically sliced it in half. Freddy held the animal up by its short tail and said it was a vole, his uncle Stosh got them in his ice fishing shanty all the time.

Bill hadn't thought about hitting the vole, or about Freddy, in years. Freddy got married right after high school, turning down a basketball scholarship to work at Fisher Body so he could buy a car and go hunting and fishing when he felt like it. Bill had been in college about two months when he heard what happened. Freddy had taken his wife bird hunting. He climbed through the fence first, in a hurry because his dog was on a scent, and when his wife climbed through she got caught in the wire or something and her gun went off. Bill knocked on Memory's door. Freddy got it square in the spine and lived to watch a lot of television, dead from the belt down. His wife divorced him before they celebrated an anniversary. The door swung open and Memory, wearing red slacks and a white satin blouse, was saying it was hot as hell in her apartment, being next to the furnace and all, and an image of Freddy Zielinski sitting in his wheelchair, a big bowl of popcorn on his lap and a beer in his hand, took its time sliding out of Bill's head.

"Are you ready for this?"

"For what?"

"Well, take your coat off and come *see*."

He followed her around the partition that hid the furnace and saw Mr. Ninner curled up on her bed.

*

On Saturday morning Bill chopped and split wood and quickly broke a sweat. He could see Jay through the kitchen window. She was baking bread. The sky was a clean bright blue, and the sun, at eleven o'clock, was casting a perfect shadow of the black walnut tree across the back yard. Mr. Ninner's path in the snow cut through the tree's highest branches. They had both taken that path to Memory's last night. She showed Bill the dish she bought for the manx's tuna. Then she gave him a present. It was a gift edition of *This Is My Beloved* by Walter Benton.

"I love those poems," she said. "I've loved them ever since I was a freshman in college. In fact, one of my cats, Wally B. Good, was sorta named after him, Walter Benton."

Bill Rau could feel that book in his pocket now as he lifted the axe. He hadn't said to Memory what he had planned to say. He swung the axe hard. Jay knocked on the window, pointing at something behind him. He turned and saw Jenny and Sophie lying in the shadowy branches beside Mr. Ninner's path, making angels. When had they come into the yard? They lay side by side, their mittens almost touching as they swept the snow to make their wings.

He raised the axe again. The large piece of oak he was working on wouldn't split, it was full of knots, and he needed an axe with a wedgehead. But he kept coming down on it, aiming for the same place. He remembered splitting wood for his grandmother after his grandfather had died. Twenty-five years ago. She had a saltblock behind her house, and the deer in her woods would come up to it. Mornings she'd sit in her dark kitchen at a window and wait for them, holding her folded hands in her lap like a little girl told to sit nice. Teasing her, Bill's father once said, "Where's your rifle, Grandma?" "Oh," she looked at him, seeing nothing funny, "you dasn't shoot those deer. Nobody dasn't." Freddy Zielinski's face, Bill remembered, was as white as hers after his accident. He never went outside anymore, he said. Bill did not want to think about him. Memory said, "The girl in my discussion group that was in your class, she'd heard you were real stuck on yourself. But she took the class anyway. She likes you. What do we discuss? Oh, lots of things. Mainly, you know, things we're not too sure of. But I'm not going to tell you her name. You might get ideas. Was I right about this here old buster, or wasn't I?"

Bill turned the piece of oak over and went at it from the other end. He could feel sweat trickle down his ribs. When the axe stuck and he had to work it back and forth to free it, he could hear the wood squeal. "Can I ask you something personal? What do you do about me, I mean about us, you know, after you get home?"

"Hey, Dad!"

Bill Rau turned. Jenny and Sophie were leaving.

"We wrote you a message. Over there," Jenny pointed.

He'd had enough chopping. He took the axe in the garage. There was a box of old magazines in the back and he buried the Benton book among them. Out in the yard he followed a series of arrows in the snow until he came to the message:

> *"Halo" said the girl.*
> *"Halo yourself" said the boy.*
> *MOOSHY!*

Bill Rau looked up from the message, toward the raspberry bushes at the back of his yard. He remembered the autumn that Jay stood beside them, waving the wind from her hair. Her hair, then, was its natural auburn color, and curly, the same color as the raspberry canes, the same color as when they met. After everything was settled, he would ask her to let that color grow back.

*

They decided to wait until after Christmas to tell Jenny their plan about moving to Spain that spring. If after three or four months there she was unhappy, they would return to the States. They would promise her that. As much as they wanted to make a clean break, they would not cause her to feel that she was "floating." But they believed that she would adapt—kids do, don't they? "And she *loves* Spanish," Jay said. "She's getting an A in it."

Despite his workout with the axe that morning, Bill was restless. Jay was too. "I'd like to quit my job next month," she said, "and just go!"

She put a leg of lamb in the oven, and they went for a walk to the public golf course.

"A line from an old story of mine has been running through my head all day," Bill said. "'We're moving—the house is old!'"

"It is! And we are!"

At the golf course they slipped through a hole in the fence, holding back the loose section of wire for each other. They walked toward the steepest fairway where some kids were sliding down or pulling toboggans and sleds back up. The kids were having a great time, and Bill and Jay stood for a minute watching them. One lad, his front teeth missing, flopped down beside his sled and blew a big pink bubble at the sky. Jay whispered, "Wouldn't you like to poke it!"

They continued walking, in a large half-circle toward the Observatory, stepping along, now and then one of them breaking into a little jog, the other running to catch up, playing a kind of tag, laughing. They were breathing hard when they got to the Observatory. Some beer cans and a wine bottle lay in front of the door. On either side of the door, imprinted in the cement, were the signs of the zodiac, and among these a display of hearts and initials in spray paint or colored chalk.

"Have you got something to write with?"

She shook her head.

He put his arms around her and kissed her forehead and both of her red cheeks. "Come skiing out here with me."

"When?"

"Christmas morning—before anybody's up."

"I love you, Billy, and that's the truth."

"I know it is."

*

Saturday night he dreamt about his father again. His father was waiting for him to bring the lawn mower across the road. He was smiling, his teeth bright as snowflakes. He stood in the front yard, beside a box, trying on all of Bill's old sweaters. Each time he put one on he got younger. Bill was hurrying across the road as fast as he could, pushing the mower ahead of him. And very glad he'd remembered to oil it! The blades struck stones and produced sparks, and his father was just old enough to walk when Bill woke up.

The frost on their bedroom windows sparkled in the moonlight. He touched Jay's warm shoulder under the covers, letting his hand rest there a few minutes. Then he got out of bed. He went across the hall to Jenny's room. She lay flat on her back with her arms outside the quilt. Carefully he put the quilt over them. In the poster above her head, a vixen and her cub looked at Bill from the entrance to their ferny den.

The top of Jenny's bookcase held her collection of small animals. He picked up the brass duck. It was cold for a moment, then warmed in his hands. He sat on the floor beside Jenny's bed, holding the duck, and tried to remember the name of the book and chart store in New York where they bought it. The store was on Water Street and afterwards he and Jay walked down to the pier and stepped aboard the *Robert Fulton*—and while a flock of gulls made slow, graceful crazy eights against the Brooklyn Bridge, he kissed her. He wanted to kiss her again like that. He wanted to bow and produce a bouquet of daisies, and walk in the park holding her hand, and read her a new poem.

Back in their room he looked at her face in the moonlight. She lay with her arms at her sides now, just like Jenny. Her face was very white, the color of snow. Bill thought of them skiing the Au Sable trail in Michigan, and coming to the place where the pines grew close together on both sides of them. Her face was the color of the snow sticking to the black bark. Then, he remembered, they came out of that thick piney place and were beside the river again, their skis making a sighing sound moving over the snow; and after a while they arrived at the log footbridge, the bridge they stood on last summer when they saw the doe. They had just got out of the river, having taken off their shoes downstream about a mile back and walked to where they stood now, their feet pink and wrinkled from the cold water, watching the doe. She was upriver and upwind of them, alert and sleek in a speckle of light, and she stood at the edge of the Au Sable taking them in, allowing them to look at her, before leaping across in a motion that made even birdsong cease for that moment. She disappeared in a thicket of aspens.

Bill leaned down and listened to Jay breathing. He kissed her hair. Then he got dressed.

The woodpile lay like a large humpbacked creature about to strike, and he regarded it, blowing into his palms. He was standing on Mr. Ninner's path. He looked at the moon through the walnut branches, then down at Jenny's and Sophie's angels; the lower rims of their wings were dipped in shadow, and in one wing—dead center—a hole, where a squirrel had gone after a buried nut. For an instant he saw the robin he'd shot flutter down from the elm beside their driveway. He was about Jenny's age, the air rifle was his Christmas present, and when he held the warm bird in his hand two or three drops of its bright blood slipped through his fingers. Ashamed, he found an empty box of kitchen matches for its coffin and buried it in the ash heap behind the garage.

He took Mr. Ninner's path to the boulevard and walked past Memory's house to the golf course. At the hole in the fence he turned around for home. In the gray morning light he remembered thinking, I will just make it hop to another branch, then he squeezed the trigger.

*

On Sunday morning — Christmas Eve — Jenny brought down her presents to her parents, Jay brought down theirs to her, plus the gift from Schooltz and Mabel, and they arranged the bright boxes under the tree.

Excited, Jay said, "Shall we open them now?"

"No, Mom. Tomorrow morning."

"Really? You can wait that long?"

"That's when you're *supposed* to open them," Jenny said sharply, her face fixed in a scowl.

"Billy's invited me to go skiing in the morning."

"Early," Bill said. "Before breakfast. Like to come along?"

63

"Well," Jenny said, softening, "I have plans in the morning."

"Oh, you do," Jay said.

"Yes, I do." Then Jenny asked her father, "What time will you be back?"

"How's ten-thirty?"

"Ten-thirty will be fine."

While splitting wood that afternoon Bill saw Ninner on the manx's path, looking in Bill's direction. He continued to split wood and she continued to stand, hesitant, and look. Finally he said, "I haven't seen him, but help yourself," sweeping his arm toward the garage. She stayed where she was.

Bill heard a woman call, "Here, Ninner! Here, baby!" The voice came from the Lithuanian woman's yard, high and extra sweet, but it wasn't hers. Ninner sat down in the path.

"Oh there you are!" Velma appeared beside the raspberry bushes; she was the Lithuanian woman's daughter who always wore black. "Come, sweet baby. Come, Ninner. Hello," she waved to Bill.

He waved back.

"Ninner," she cooed, "*please* come to me."

The cat looked at Bill, at the garage, then licked a paw. She wasn't moving anywhere.

"Oh you funny girl." Velma came quickly into the yard, pinching her black shawl together with one hand and lifting her billowy skirts with the other. She was short, barely five feet, and wore ballet slippers. Making a fresh path in the snow, she sank halfway to her knees. She laughed and said something musical in Lithuanian.

After picking up the cat and rubbing cheeks with it, she said, "You're going to have a nice fire?"

"Yes."

"So are we!" She smiled her big dreamy smile.

"You look happy," Bill said.

"Oh I am bursting! Bursting!"

He was hoping she would tell him why, but she was already turning to go.

"Take the path," Bill suggested. "It'll be easier."

"Thank you, yes. Bye-bye." She hurried away, her full black skirts flying.

Velma was the Lithuanian woman's youngest daughter, and the only one in that family whom Bill had ever really exchanged words with, other than greetings. But they never said very much because she always seemed in the middle of something, a little chore like fetching a single tomato from her mother's garden on the other side of the raspberry bushes, or fetching the cat, these small missions incidental parts of a dance, it seemed, that she must suddenly make across the yard and back, or burst. And yet he felt that if they had the right words to say—words to go with her wide dreamy smile—they might talk for hours. Once he did have a word ready—*burd*—which he'd discovered some years after he began calling Jenny "Bird." He planned to ask Velma if she didn't think it amazing that the nickname he had given his daughter, but spelled with a *u,* meant "maiden," and was labeled *poetic* in the dictionary. But when she appeared again he couldn't bring the word out. She surprised him, she always did—she was like a little fiction only partially formed. Her smile seemed so at odds with her somber clothes. And she wore a lot of clothes, layers, even in summer; and they always seemed too large for her, as if they weren't hers at all. She lived in Minneapolis. He had no idea what she did there and could not bring himself to ask. Velma was about thirty. She and her two sisters, who lived in Omaha, came to visit their mother often. Their father had long been dead. The Raus had never seen him. Perhaps, as Jay said, he was killed by the Communists. After twelve years of living within fifty yards of this family, Bill and Jay knew practically nothing about them.

Bill went back to splitting wood. He must remember, he thought, not to call Jenny "Bird" anymore; just recently she decided that she was too old for it. He formed a picture of Velma and Ninner in front of a good fire; she spoke to the cat in Lithuanian—rich, mysterious sounds that meant everything and nothing. He also pictured the manx, sprawled on Memory's bed until she dragged him off by his front paws, then dropped him on an oversize pillow. *His* pillow, she said. Up close, his face looked mauled, beaten. An old scar lay on his snout like a worm. When Memory stroked his belly, an immense groan of satisfaction, almost human, issued from his throat.

"You want to hear what I'm going to call him?" she said.

"His name is Mr. Ninner," Bill said.

"Not anymore. From now on it's Shakespeare!"

The back door opened and Jay came out. Her eyes were red. Bill said, "What's wrong?"

She shrugged her shoulders.

He pulled a big piece of hickory off the pile, then set it on end. "Here," he said, handing her the axe, "give it a whack."

"I'd just cut my foot off."

"What's the matter?"

"Jenny."

"What about Jenny?" He took back the axe.

"She's critical of everything I do lately."

"Like what?"

"I asked her to pick up her room and she said I had stringy hair."

"She was teasing you."

"It isn't funny."

"Who's laughing?" Bill smiled.

"I asked if she wanted to help dress the turkey and she gave me that long disgusted-with-everything sigh."

"Didn't you have that sigh when you were thirteen?"

"She says she stays in her room so much because we're boring—all we do is take walks and read."

"I never hear her talk like that."

"She doesn't like me."

"She bought you a present."

"She hates me, Billy."

"Stop it."

"I *know* she does."

"Listen, the mister give me strict orders about this wood," Bill said. "He sees me with the scullery maid he'll box me ears."

"Last night I dreamt I was in my coffin."

Bill laid the axe against the woodpile and put his arm around his wife.

"The lid was in place and they lowered me in the hole. But I was still breathing." She started to cry.

"Come on, baby."

"She won't *forgive* me, Billy."

The Raus' upstairs bathroom had two small windows that faced the back yard. Days later in a motel in Kansas City or

Tulsa or Santa Fe something slid into place in Bill's head and he saw Jenny looking down on them from a corner of one of those windows, her face behind the overhanging icicles a pink smear.

✳

She was sitting on her bed, adding photos to the album.

"Mind if I join you?" Bill said.

She shook her head.

Bill sat on the bed and looked at the pictures with her. Jenny kept all of their loose pictures in a big shoebox; from time to time she would go through the box and find ones she liked for the album.

"I'm way behind," she said. "I don't even have last winter in." She held up two photographs. "Which do you like better—this one, or this one?"

They were shots of Jenny with her dog Missy in the yard. In one she was hugging the German shepherd's head; in the other Missy lay on her back, paws limp, and Jenny was rubbing snow on her belly. They were taken last December, just before the Raus left for Michigan.

"These are both keepers," her father said.

"We should have taken her with us," Jenny said.

"On the plane? You know how she would've tolerated *that*. Besides, Sophie took very good care of her."

"Do you like this one?"

It was a picture of Jenny and her mother on the swings in the park across the lake from their cottage. They had all walked over one afternoon, visiting fishermen at their shanties along the way. In the picture Bill caught them at the far point of their arc, about to swing back—their mouths surprised and their cheeks flaming.

"You guys know how to have a good time. Put this one in for sure."

"How about this one? Are my eyes funny?"

"Let ze doktor eggsamin."

"I didn't even know you were taking it. I was writing in my diary."

"Your eyes are beautiful. Another must."

"I'm behind in my diary too."

"Not easy being thirteen."

"Don't tease, Dad."

"Hey, I just got a brilliant idea. How would you like to warm an old man's heart?"

"Meaning yours."

"Meaning mine. Come skiing on the public links tomorrow morning. It would please your mother too."

"Well," she hesitated, "I *do* sort of have something planned."

"In the early hours?"

"It's a surprise." She worked at keeping a straight face.

"Ah, I get it. Well, maybe in the afternoon?"

"Maybe. How about this one?" she handed her father a picture that she had taken.

Jay and Bill had just arrived at the dock after a morning swim last summer. It was a stunning morning—a cumulus of light blue mist rose up from the lake directly in front of the cottage—the soul of some wonderful underwater sky come forth—and the water all around the cumulus was a delicate piney green. Jay and Bill stood on the dock in that rich color—

her head tilted, smiling—and she never looked lovelier, he thought. He had a finger in his ear and his eyes were crossed.

"Who *is* that clown?" Bill said.

"That was the most beautiful day we ever had," Jenny said. The deep appreciation in her voice shamed him. He put a thumb over his mugging face and kept it there until the next picture.

*

Christmas morning Bill and Jay got up at seven. The night before he taped their skis and poles in two bundles, and now they carried them to the golf course. It was quiet and cold out, the sky was changing from dark to gray. Their boots squeaked as they walked. They slipped through the hole in the fence, put on the skis, and started for the fairway where the kids went down on their sleds. The snow was crusty, and randomly the ground was pure ice, making the skiing graceless and difficult. The climb to the top of the fairway was especially hard, and several times they lost their balance and fell to their knees. But finally they got to the top. The sliding area lay slick and shiny all the way down.

"It'll be some ride," Bill said.

"You first."

"If I don't make it, tell Mother Rau I went with a full stomach."

He pushed off, stayed in a crouch, and almost got down without falling. A sudden dip near the end turned him over.

"Are you all right?" Jay called.

"Fine!"

She came down and the same dip got her.

"My God!" she laughed, lying in a sprawl.

"Break anything?"

"About half."

"The teenager will enjoy hearing about it."

"That rascal. I wonder what she's planning?"

"A treat. Come on. Let's tame this joint."

But they didn't tame anything. The snow was just too hard or the ground icy or in spots bare. They didn't give up, though. They made a complete circle of the course, stopping at the Observatory. The sun lay almost above the trees then, and when Jay faced it Bill could see bits of sparkle in the frosty down on her cheeks.

"You look wonderful."

"I feel good, Billy."

He did too. They took off their skis and sat on the Observatory steps to rest before going home. Someone had cleaned up the trash, but the hearts with their initials remained.

"Maybe I shouldn't tell you this," Jay said.

"Tell me what?"

"I've been breaking a lot of dishes lately." She gave Bill a sidelong smile.

"What's the joke?"

"Oh, I don't know. But that's supposed to be a sure sign."

"A sure sign of what?"

"You really don't know?"

"Tell me."

"That you're pregnant."

"Jay—"

"But that's the *only* sign. So far."

She stood up, hands on her hips.

"Well sir," she said, gazing out over the course, "I thought we were splendid today. Which gives me a splendid idea." She turned to him and said quickly, "Billy, let's take a week and slip off to Michigan."

He shook his head: he'd been thinking the same thing.

"Don't you want to?" she said.

"Of course I do," he smiled. "That's a date."

Taping the skis and poles together, he heard her say—more to herself than to him—"See? I can bounce back."

They started for home. It was about ten o'clock by the sun and they were hungry. On the boulevard a jogger passed them, his mouth covered with a surgical mask, and then a car with four very old people in it drove by slowly, and that was all the traffic for about ten blocks.

"How would you like," Bill said, "a big bowl of oatmeal garnished with raisins, walnuts, and sliced banana, sweetened with a splash of gen-u-ine maple syrup, and maybe a poached egg on the side?"

"Cream on the oatmeal?"

"Without question."

"Sausage?"

"A succulent patty or two, with pepper."

"You'll fix?"

"It's practically done."

They heard a siren start up.

"Oh dear," Jay said. "Do you think those old people are in an accident?"

"They're probably in church."

A second siren joined the first.

"What a rotten time for a fire."

The sirens seemed to feed off each other, building up and up until suddenly they broke and whined to a quick stop. The fire was nearby. Traffic increased, and here and there a man stepped out on his front porch. Bill remembered how his father always stood at the door when a siren went off. A police car went by, fast, and turned at the Raus' corner. Bill and Jay started running even before they saw the smoke. He threw down his skis and ran and saw all of the porch screens knocked out and firemen with hoses pouring water through the French doors and spraying the roof, and then somebody grabbed him and Bill pushed the man away and two more got him and Jay was screaming Jenny's name.

3

He couldn't sleep. He got up and found a light, and stood facing the dead television set. Though he didn't want to watch it, he searched in his pants for a quarter anyway, for something to do. That gave him another idea. He sat on the floor and arranged his coins and bills in stacks and piles, as he did when he was a kid counting the contents of his pig. He counted the money three times, got three different figures. Then he looked at the picture on the wall—a thin stick of a man on a burro, in orange and purple velvet. Bill could see that its purpose was to complement the orange carpet, the purple curtains, and the purple chair.

Now he was aware of traffic noises on the highway, trucks grinding up the grade from the intersection, shifting, shifting again, and going out toward the desert flats his bus was heading for yesterday when he got off. He hadn't planned on staying two nights in that room, but there he was, with the thin orange man on the purple burro.

Bill Rau stood up, walked around the room a few times, then sat at the desk, where his bottle was. He saw a ladybug on the lampshade. He gave her his thumb and she got on. He bent his fingers, keeping them together, and she walked across the nails to the little finger, then up to the first joint and back over the other joints to the thumb again. There she hesitated. "Try a new direction," he said. Down the thumb to the back of his wrist she went; then through the hairs and around to the blue veins on the inside. "Try the palm," he said. The palm it was. But she didn't seem to care for that—maybe the lifeline pinched her—and she made fast for the thumb, perching on its tip a moment, quivering her wings, before flying back to the lampshade. He picked up the bottle and poured himself a drink.

It was Saturday night. That was the night for his father's bath. He liked Bill to wash his back.

"What are those red dots?"

"Oh, special freckles. Scrub hard, son."

In the tub his father seemed a lot smaller than when he had his work clothes on; and because he never took off his shirt outdoors the skin on his back was the color of a fish's belly. But his neck and face were always brown, even in winter, and his hands, big-knuckled and rough, were even browner. The pencil he wore over his ear made a thick mark on his white sideburn. That would be washed off on Saturday night. By Monday night Bill could see the mark start to come back, and during the week it grew darker and thicker.

"How did you get them, those dots?"

"When I miss and hit my finger, I get one. That's how you keep track."

"But I never see you miss. Never."

His father just laughed.

The next few times that Bill hit his thumb driving a nail, he ran in the house and took off his shirt and looked in the mirror.

No red dots. When he told his father about it, his father said they were keeping track underneath, and would surface when he started to shave.

Saturday nights in summer they all went out for ice cream. It was a little shack of a place that also sold milk in glass jugs with the cream up at the top; Bill's mother would save the cream for hot oatmeal or coffee. They would all go in the shack, except for his father, who stayed behind the wheel, and get their double-dip cones (his father always had vanilla), and then go for a ride with all the windows down. They would go to look at nice houses whose lawns were like carpets, and Bill's mother would point and whisper she wanted *that* kind of brick, *those* kind of features, and his father, eating his cone, shifting, letting the clutch out so you'd never even feel the car jerk, wearing his slippers for relief from his work shoes all week, would nod and maybe say, "We can do that," or maybe offer another idea.

"I just don't want a box, Alec."

"It won't be."

"I want a pretty house."

And in the back seat Bill and Helen and Andy would have to behave, because this was a *nice* neighborhood, their mother would say, putting on fresh lipstick and then making a perfect copy of her lips on the napkin from the ice cream shack. And Helen, licking slow to make her cone outlast everybody else's, would say, "Yumm," to tease her brothers.

"How about a bite, Bug," their father would say.

"No."

"I'll give you a smooch?"

"You *scratch*," she'd say, giggling, and he'd laugh and take them home.

Saturday nights in winter Bill's mother made popcorn and hot chocolate, and his father would spread over the kitchen table the different house plans he'd cut from the newspaper. He was going to borrow the best ideas from each one, he said, and build them all a house that wasn't a box. And then he'd wink at Bill or Helen or Andy, but for their mother to see too.

"I don't trust you, Alec. It'll be just like all those cottages your dad built—boxes. I want a *ranch*-style. With a stone fireplace. And cupboards where I can *put* things! Oh Alec, I just want a pretty house."

One Saturday night when he took the plans from the kitchen drawer, everyone saw that they had been scribbled all over with crayons, and one was ripped. Helen pointed at Andy and said, "You wrecked them! You wrecked them!" and he started to cry.

Bill's father picked up Andy and sat him on his knee. "Didn't wreck anything, did you, Gumper. Fact is, Bug, he's giving us ideas for the painting and such. And this one here"—he slid the ripped plan away from the others—"wasn't much to begin with." He wadded it into a ball and set it on Andy's head, and Bill's mother dabbed his wet cheeks with a dish towel.

Saturday nights when the snow had gone and they could see buds on the grape vines out back, Bill's father would spade in the garden until it got dark, turning up worms that Bill would pull out slowly and put in the can that Andy was holding. Helen would push her doll on the swing by the pear tree, watching her brothers warily—because once, changing her doll's diaper, she touched a night crawler on its belly. Bill's mother hugged her and said her brother was naughty, and asked him, "Please, Billy." His father said, "Save those for your hook, son." His parents glanced at each other, trying to look stern, though he could see their eyes weren't stern at all; and Helen, her mouth bunched tight and her chin trembling, remembered the *worst* thing he did to her doll, which was to cut the cry thing out when he wanted to be a doctor. Bill's father said he'd have to bust his pig to buy her a new one—but Helen didn't want a new doll, she wanted *Brenda*. So his mother put the doll's cry thing back in her stomach and sewed her up and Bill apologized and tried, as he promised, not to experiment on Helen's toys anymore, or tease her. But he couldn't resist just one crawler one Saturday night in the spring when his father spaded the garden and everything smelled so alive.

Bill was in high school when his mother's dream house was ready. It was toward the end of summer, football practice had started, and pouring another drink he could see himself walking in the country, walking to their new home, his cleats tied together over his shoulder. His father said they would be pouring the basement floor after dinner. Uncle Jack would help them. Bill's legs were sore from practice, but he was excited too, because the basement floor was the last big job. Except for that and some finish work, everything was done. Everything inside, that is. They still had the yard to level off and the trees to plant.

"I won't see these trees high as they'll get," his father said, and his mother said, "Alec, you're just barely forty, stop that kind of talk."

But before they planted the trees that fall, going up north in the truck and digging them out of Grandma's woods and wrapping their roots in wet burlap, they had to gather in the basement with hoes and shovels and wait for the Ready Mix man to send his concrete down the shoot.

Down it came and they started spreading it. "Should be a lot soupier," his father said, and he yelled to Bill's mother, who stood on the stairs, worrying, "Get the hose and get Gumper and Helen down here, and grab a shovel too!"

So they all went to work on that giant mound of concrete that was starting to set—Andy spraying it with the hose, Helen chopping at it with a hoe, and Bill and his father and mother hauling shovelfuls to Uncle Jack who, on his knees, troweled it with a two-by-four. "Don't let it freeze on us, Gumper," his father kept saying, cheering them on, and the sweat rolled off their chins and glistened in his father's and Uncle Jack's whiskers. "I hafta go!" Andy cried, and Bill's father yelled, "Pee on the pile, nobody's watching!"

They worked until past midnight, but they got it done. The floor lay level and grainily smooth, and exhausted and sore as they were, they sat on the stairs like a small faithful following long after the event is over, and looked at their work, admiring it, drinking beer and pop and laughing at how hard they'd labored, until Andy and Helen were fast asleep and Bill's father and Uncle Jack carried them up to the new bedrooms which smelled of fresh lumber and window caulking and wood paste and all the slow summer afternoons that Bill remembered building deserts in the sawdust under the big blue buzzsaw in his Grandpa's lumberyard.

He turned off the light and returned to bed. He heard the trucks grinding and shifting, and then he heard a burst of applause. Behind the orange man on the wall. Applause, laughter, and then a man's voice sounding as if it came up from the bottom of a barrel, his mouth full of soft food or cotton, stuttering . . . followed by squeals of laughter . . . followed by a drumroll . . . followed by moaning singers whose mouths might also be full of soft food or cotton, coming up from the bottom of the stutterer's barrel . . .

Bill thought of the man in the bar in Kansas City who talked to the rack of Beef Jerkies, and he didn't know if he was going to laugh or get out of bed and pour whiskey over his head and hop up and down like a monkey. He felt seized by his bones, which were controlled by something outside of himself, shaking him. His bones wanted to throw off his flesh, throw out his guts. To protect himself from coming apart he brought his knees up and hugged them, and lay in the tightest ball he could make. Then he started to count—by fives. He got to five hundred when the man talking to the Beef Jerkies came back into his head.

The man had the kind of face he'd seen before, many times, usually around run-down gas stations—long sideburns razored clean at the jaw, a sharp nose with a scab on the bridge. His jaw—the side toward Bill—was swollen purple, as if the wisdom tooth were on fire, or someone had clobbered him. He stared at the Beef Jerkies and said—the words whiny, scratchy—"They found my wife's body out in Hollywood, California, last month." His nostrils flared as if the Beef Jerkies had committed an offense. "Bowling, everybody'd watch her," he said. "Home, she'd walk back and forth in front of the mirror, all dressed up. She wanted to be a movie star." He paused; his eyes reminded Bill of the suckers he speared in his grandfather's creek in the spring. "She was dead two days before anybody found her." Bill got off his stool and left the bar. Outside he remembered his bag and went back for it. The man was still talking to the Beef Jerkies, ". . . she was the most decent woman I ever knew . . ."

Beyond the wall the moaning singers had stopped. Bill heard "The Star-Spangled Banner." Then it was quiet except for the trucks grinding and shifting, and a dog that barked a few times. Bill's room, even in the dark, seemed to get smaller and smaller. He continued to lie in the tight ball of himself. He smelled old sweat, stale tobacco smoke. He tried to think of being outside . . . and after a while remembered lying in his tent beside the Sturgeon River up north in Michigan the summer after he graduated from high school. He was alone, on a camping trip before starting college, and lying in the tent he listened to the river wash past the boulders a few feet away. In his tight ball in the motel room he remembered how pleasant that sound was, and he made a large place in his head for the boulders and the water flowing past them in white curves and skips in the moonlight. He tried to follow that rhythm out of himself. Then something interfered with the rhythm, a scratching or pawing close to the tent. A coon, he thought. He slapped the tent's roof, but he really didn't care if a coon was out there—he had all of his food inside. In the morning, a few feet from the tent, he found the foreleg of a calf.

That was near Wolverine. Or Rondo. Or Vanderbilt. He couldn't remember exactly. He started to count again—by twos—and by concentrating on the numbers he was able to let go of his legs and straighten them. When he reached one hundred he had his feet on the floor. Then he was standing up, and walking, stepping on his stacks and piles of money, trying to remember. Porcupine Lake, Kidney Lake, Dog Lake. He could see those lakes but he couldn't see himself on them or beside them. All he could see were the lonesome shacks along the old highway, their cheap brown Insulbrick peeling off, and the acres of young Christmas trees planted in tidy rows on the sandy hillsides . . . but he couldn't remember what he was near when the calf's leg was left beside his tent. The Sturgeon River—but where! Then he thought of his uncle Herman, who said, "Maybe he needs a bell tied around his neck."

Bill was fourteen, finally old enough to go deer hunting in the St. Helen's woods up north. Where his father had gone for years with his brothers and uncles—and where, if you got lost, you might never be found, his cousin Robert said.

Bill knew about those woods from the summers when they visited Uncle Herman who lived in Rose City, about twenty miles away. But this was different; this wasn't taking a walk in the woods with your father and mother and little sister and brother and sitting in a birch grove to eat the picnic your mother had packed.

So the first day he stayed where his father had put him and waited for his buck to come down the hill he sat facing. But nothing came down, not even a doe, and he wanted to go deeper in the woods, walk around, feel that he was hunting. Sitting by the camp fire that night he asked his father to let him *go in* like Robert could, who was only a year older than Bill. But he didn't ask when Robert or Uncle Raymond or any of the others were around, and maybe that's why, after a while, his father said all right.

In the morning they talked over how the old fire lanes ran in a grid, dividing the woods into squares, and how each square was a hundred acres or more—plenty of room to get all the walking in he needed. "Just don't cross a lane," his father warned. They walked along one for a while to get a feel for it. The fire lanes had been cut in the thirties by the Civilian Conservation Corps to help contain forest fires and Bill could see, as his father pointed to all the new growth, that he'd have to pay attention.

They came to a clearing, and Bill saw beyond it where the fire lane picked up again. His father let him go on alone.

Bill crossed the clearing and entered the farther woods. His boots were new, his cap was new, and in the pocket of his father's old hunting coat the two extra shells clicked together as he walked. An apple, a cheese sandwich, and a Hershey bar were in the other big pocket.

He ate the apple first, walking along . . . tossing the core at a big hollow charred stump to warn whatever was hiding inside to stay inside. He kept close to the fire lane. He planned to follow it around the square he was in and end up back near camp. When the sun was near ten o'clock he sat against a birch and waited for his buck to come across an open sandy place. Bill ate the sandwich and wished he had another. He thought about having to drag his buck back to camp, if he got one. But after an hour or so he had seen only a couple of chipmunks and some blackbirds gliding overhead.

Cold, he continued walking. He crossed two or three more open sandy places and skirted a cedar swamp, losing the fire lane then finding it again. Now he was heating up in the heavy clothes and realized he was walking too fast. But he didn't want to get caught out there in the dark. He sat down to cool off and eat the candy bar, careful to point the rifle away from his feet. His father knew a careless man who'd lost three toes.

Finally Bill decided to retrace his steps, because the sun was past noon and he knew it got dark fast in the woods. He recrossed all the sandy places and went around the swamp, but he couldn't find the fire lane . . . and the sun was touching the tree tops. He walked faster, thinking about the campfire and the stew the men would make . . . opening large cans of tomatoes and beef and potatoes and dumping everything into a big pan and standing around watching it bubble. Once he thought he saw a bear and almost fired, but it was only the bushy root end of a tree pushed over. "Never shoot a bear in the nose, you'll only make him mad," his uncle Raymond said.

Bill walked and walked and everything looked familiar and nothing did. He saw the stuffed, snarling bobcat in his grandfather's lumberyard, on the wall above the safe. What if one decided to jump him? He kept his finger on the trigger. He was sweating. He knew he could work up a sweat and then when he couldn't walk anymore the sweat would freeze. But he knew enough to keep his coat on, and walk slower, and keep the sun in front of him. But it was almost down and twice, three times he passed what looked like the same big charred stump . . . and the trees became darker and thicker . . . and he now believed the bobcats and bears were waiting for him to lie down and fall asleep. His finger was numb. He kept biting it. If anything leaped out in front of him he had to be ready . . .

Then he heard them, their walking noises. He jerked up the rifle. But he couldn't get his cold finger over the trigger, and then they spoke, two men.

They drove him into Rose City, to his uncle Herman's place. Aunt Lavina gave him a piece of cold pork for the ride back. In the truck Uncle Herman didn't say much. Bill felt dizzy.

At camp a big fire was blazing. Herman told Bill's father, "He came in looking like a wet rabbit." While Bill ate a plate of stew, Robert said to him, "Your dad used up all his shells firing at the sky every two minutes, and had to borrow more." To Bill, later, his father just said, "You stayed out a little late, son." The others didn't say anything.

Next morning before Bill and his father left their tent, Bill asked if he could go out by himself again. His father said nothing. They drank their coffee, watching the others go off, then they walked along the fire lane for a ways.

"I know I can follow it this time," Bill said.

"Are you sure?"

Bill said he was.

"All right," his father said.

In his motel room Bill Rau sat at the desk with his bottle, seeing again, almost smelling, that fresh piney dawn with the light breaking through the trees, and hearing his father say, "Have you got your tag?" Bill showed him the metal tag you fastened in the deer's antlers to claim it; but they both knew that bagging a buck was not the main business now. The main—the only—business now was to take a simple walk in the woods in late autumn and not get lost again. Bill wanted to put the memory of it aside, just have a drink from his bottle and become sleepy and sleep, and not dream—or if he had to dream, let it be about strangers who didn't mean anything to him; but he was already following the fire lane, and then not following it, and the sun was going down and he was frightened all over again, crying, feeling empty and sick in his guts, and then seeing the camp fire and wanting to shout *I did it!* Only it wasn't their camp—strangers again—and again he was driven to Herman's. And again Herman had to deliver him, saying nothing during the ride. And when they arrived at the camp Herman did not even get out of his truck for a schnapps—he just rolled down his window and told the others, "Maybe he needs a bell tied around his neck."

In the morning they drove home. Bill's father put on his hunting clothes twice more that Bill knew of—both times to sit over a hole in the ice in a shanty on Saginaw Bay, for perch.

*

He felt boxed in. He found his shoes and carried a glass of bourbon outside and looked at the sky. It was the new year but that was the same sky. Bill Rau drank to the same sky, to the stars, to the blinker light at the intersection, to a truck grinding its gears and going away.

His glass was empty. But why wasn't he drunk? He wanted to get on his bus drunk in the morning and ride drunk into Mexico and buy a big sombrero and get under it and sleep. That's why he bought this ticket in Kansas City! He could have bought a different ticket but he didn't, he bought this one! And whose fine brain was it anyway that thought up putting a God damn picnic table between a motel sign and a highway?!

Bill sat at the picnic table and raised his empty glass to another truck going by. He and Jay were planning to go to Mexico, one of these days, but they never did. In Detroit, on their third date, he said, "How does Mexico sound?" He hadn't even kissed her yet! Not even a good-night peck on the cheek! "I'd like that," she said, and his heart started skipping or knocking, making it hard for him to walk. They were heading toward the Bagel Shop on Woodward Avenue in a warm October rain. How could they eat anything? How could they *not* eat anything! Two big pieces of apple strudel, still steaming from the oven, were set before them, and they practically fell on them, keeping their lips and tongues occupied, pacifying them, burning them, until later.

"Maybe we ought to get married before we go?" he said.

She smiled, nodding. "My father would like that too."

And Bill Rau at his picnic table on the edge of the desert remembered how sweetly the time passed before they did get married, three months later. Meeting her for lunch at the Hotel Belcrest near the Wayne State campus (their waiter was always slick Eli, whose latest girlfriend worked in the circulation department of Bill's newspaper) . . . seeing the Bolshoi Ballet, the first time for both of them . . . driving over to Canada to polka with farmers in country bars near the river, then coming back to the carriage house apartment he was subletting from a designer at Chrysler and making omelets at midnight . . . listening to Jay practice reading Thomas Wolfe's "Young and Drunk and Twenty" for her speech class—and suddenly the mouse they'd heard scratching the wall *appeared*, and sat up, and listened to her too! And when they told friends about it their friends would smile and nod at this obviously romantic vision. But it was true, they both saw him sitting up like a little gentleman, ears erect and holding his paws at Jay's tentative rendering of Wolfe's booming cry, "You are a poet and the world is yours!" But if no one quite believed them that was all right too, because then the mouse was theirs, along with the immense and light-limbed magic of their own drunkenness. And if they were not reeling through moon-whitened streets shouting their wild joy and laying claim to more than the expanse they felt in their breasts, they did believe, as Wolfe did, that they were limitless and would never die.

But Bill Rau at his picnic table was not drunk, didn't *feel* drunk, remembering that beautiful drunkenness, and fetched more bourbon from his room. Returning outside he said, "A table for one, Eli! By the highway's fine!"

She lived with three other girls in an apartment near the Wayne State campus. One day all four got trapped in the old elevator. The fire department rescued them after a couple of hours, and Bill wrote the story—"MISS FREEDOM STUCK IN LIFT."

A week later he called her for a date.

"My roommates and I are mad at you."

"Why?" But Bill could guess.

"Ever since your story came out we've been getting . . . well—"

"Kook calls."

"Yes."

"Price you pay for being a beauty queen."

"I'm not a beauty queen. Miss Freedom Festival was based on other things—like citizenship and scholarship."

Uh-huh, he thought. "What about Miss Greater Detroit Hardware Dealers Association? Did I get that right?"

"My agency arranged that, but I'm not doing conventions anymore. In fact I'm through modeling."

"I called to ask you out for a beer. But I just remembered, you're underage."

"I've got I.D."

False I.D., local beauty contests, businessmen's conventions—oh, he knew all about her. Wasn't he a novelist?

No, he was an ordinary reporter, bored with writing the same story over and over, wondering if he *could* write a real book, and troubled by Annie. Rolling up those sensible blue eyes in the well-scrubbed suburb where she taught second grade, she wanted to know when he was going to mature. When he was going to stop wasting his time in dives with his aimless musician friends, when he was going to stop acting silly like Mike Callahan. "You have a good position—and you know it," she'd say, neat and professional and arranged. But so creamy underneath that he would drive back to the city in a heady buzz of fermentation. A few days later, sober, angry that his real book was not going anywhere, he would consider giving himself to the military (it appeared unlikely that, at twenty-four, he would be drafted, especially since the volunteer rate at his board in Flint was high) or he would call up Rhonda LeClair, née Wnuk. But, now he had another model to call, Miss Jay Schooltz—what a funny name!—and he knew all about models.

Lay her? The first date he couldn't even find the courage to kiss her. "When I was sixteen I thought modeling was *so* glamorous. It's about as glamorous as a Jucit blender—which is what I carried around for an entire day recently, like a baby."

The second date he held her hand, taking it as they skipped down the steps of the Art Institute, where they'd gone to do research for her Humanities paper. Standing in front of the swarming fat couples of Brueghel's *Wedding Dance,* Bill thought of long, cool Rhonda and her bobbed nose whose tip was now dead, and of how much more of herself she was willing to give up to become what Miss Jay Schooltz no longer cared about. Miss Jay Schooltz, visibly intact, was studying the cod-pieced farmers and their bulbous-nosed ample women that they, the two of them, were seeing Brueghel see—and seeing that *that* was the point. "He likes them, really likes them, doesn't he?" she said, and Bill knew he would never put his hands on her as he had on Rhonda LeClair, née Wnuk, or have to be careful around the middle of her face.

Lay her? Coming out of the Bagel Shop into that warm October rain, his tongue raw from the hot strudel and his gut a boil of butterflies, he walked her the eight or nine blocks to her apartment like someone pursued and there, at the outside entrance, kissed her good-night. Just once.

Then couldn't find his car, walking—yes, on air!—back and forth in front of her building.

"Billy!" She was calling down from her fourth-floor window.

He waved. "I think my car's been swiped!"

"You parked it over by Hilberry Theatre!"

"That's right! We saw *Charley's Aunt!*" He'd completely forgot. "Did you like it!"

"Yes!"

"Can I come up!"

"Yes!"

She buzzed him in and he ran up the four flights, not that he didn't trust the elevator, but he was in a hurry.

Did it really happen like that?

And did he now rush home after work, avoiding the after-hours joints where his pals played, to soak his head in a sink of cold water to wash the who's, what's, and where's out of it, then sit at the kitchen table too happy and loose in his own joints to write anything, let alone the lonely-precious stuff he had been writing?

And did he feel a fizzy, goofy combustion just below his scalp when it came time to journey to Pontiac, to Aunt Victoria's doilied parlor, to be examined by the family?

And did he eat all of his boiled chicken?

At first Bill didn't know quite what to make of that sober group. Except for Jay's father, who was called Schooltz by everyone (as if he were a handyman), none of them looked under seventy, they all followed Bill with magnified, owl-like eyes from behind exactly the same style of rimless glasses, and only one, Great-aunt Liddy visiting from Denver, deviated from what seemed a strict Fundamentalist perch: she wore rich circles of red rouge on her sharp cheekbones and chain-smoked cork-tipped cigarettes. At eighty-five she was also the oldest. There was no drink on the table but water, accompanied by the boiled chicken, boiled potatoes, some limp off-brownish boiled roots that once likely were carrots, and a white ceramic squirrel, about an inch high, that produced salt from its tail. Bill could hear throats swallow and stomachs commence digestion. And under the table he felt Jay squeeze his knee.

These were her mother's people, the survivors, for that lady had died delivering Jay. Victoria, James, Regina, Richard, Mary, and Henry—six aunts and uncles royally named and pale as the boiled chicken they chewed—and Great-aunt Liddy (a former dance hall floozy?) who pulled a lavender sachet out of her sleeve and dropped it down her bosom during the Jello dessert. "It keeps me fresh!" she declared, and all of her people pretended not to hear. Victoria, James, Regina, Richard, Mary, Henry—and Elizabeth, the baby, the only one who married.

What a strange family. Jay had told Bill that they all seven grew up on a farm in southern Indiana, and one by one came north to be bank clerks, accountants, bookkeepers. Her mother, however, had worked in a flower shop . . . and married a mechanic. Bill wondered if the pretty woman in the oval frame on the whatnot behind the piano was Elizabeth. (Except for the helmet-style short black hair, she looked a lot like Jay.) But he did not ask. He did ask about the photo on the piano—and the women proudly said it was Jay, on the night of her prom.

As for the mechanic Schooltz, he understood what the occasion called for. He followed Bill and Jay out to the car afterwards like a big friendly bear and produced a bottle and glass.

"How many fingers?"

"One," Bill said. Jay had the same.

"I'll have a couple myself," he said. He raised the glass to them with his left hand (missing its third and fourth digits), and winked.

Riding back to Detroit, Bill said, "Did I pass?"

"My dad likes you. The others will too."

"I like him. I was wondering how he and your mother met."

"He said they were lonely and poor and lucky." Jay smiled to herself. After a while she said, quietly, "But when I was growing up I never appreciated him. I was convinced I'd been adopted—or found on a doorstep. Isn't that awful? And how I hated it when Aunt Victoria came to school for parent-teacher conferences! I'd always try to be sick those days. She was so *old*. Everyone assumed she was my mother, and I'd have to say, 'She's my *aunt*.' But the worst day of my life was when George Bessie went around telling about my dad's fingers. For a long time I was ashamed to be even seen with him. So when

I saw the ad for modeling school—I was twelve—I cut it out and put it in my Bible, and some nights I even prayed to it. That probably doesn't make any sense to you."

A few days later, on the phone, Bill told his mother he was bringing home a girl for them to meet. She said, "Where's Annie?"

"In Birmingham, I guess."

"In Birmingham? What's wrong with her?"

"Nothing."

"She's a nice girl."

"I know she is, Mom. So's Jay. You'll like her."

"What does she eat?"

"Anything. Can you make golamki?"

"I *always* make it for you, when don't I make it? I mean is she fussy, this one? Annie wasn't fussy. Why don't you bring her anymore?"

"Jay's part Polish, Mom," he fibbed. "At least she sure looks it, you know how beautiful Polish girls are, and you're going to love her!"

"First you said like her. We'll see. Are you coming for church? We go to ten o'clock Mass now. That's too early for you, I suppose."

"Golamki, OK? And the potatoes?"

"Don't you want to say hello to Dad? I'll call him, he's outside."

"Can't, I'm on a story. See you Sunday after church."

When they arrived his mother had the works in the oven—czarnina, pierogi, golamki—and a ham "in case your girlfriend, I mean this Jay, don't like the others," she whispered when Bill's father took Jay outside to look at his trees.

They liked her right away, especially his father and Helen and Andy. His mother was a little slower to warm up. Partly because of her loyalty to Annie, partly because that was her way with any girl Bill dated, at first. But when Jay began eating and praising the food, there was no contest.

"This soup is *won*derful, Mrs. Rau."

"Oh, you probably got just as good, or maybe better, at home," she said, and he realized that his "part Polish" lie had landed.

"No—never!"

"Well, blood soup *is* a little trouble. And some people don't like it—the idea, you know? But your mother made golamki— everybody makes golamki—"

Bill Rau slowly stood up with his empty glass and said to the desert sky, throwing his arms out wide, "*Every*body makes golamki!" Then he gazed around the picnic table, bowing elaborately five times from the waist as if to five companions. Then he sat down. "Please, continue eating," he said. He remembered how they all applauded the pumpkin pie his mother brought out for desert (the pumpkin had come from his father's garden). "And I think we topped it with whipped, not ice, cream," he said. "And—if I am not mistaken—Helen said she wanted pie at her wedding, instead of cake." What else did anyone say? He couldn't recall. He could only remember that Jay beamed at his family for all she was worth, and the message was sweet and clear.

That night she stayed with him in the carriage house. They lay in each other's arms as easily as nature or God or the Primal Force allows, and said a lot of private things, and heard a boat signal from time to time (his bedroom window faced the Detroit River a long block away), and smelled the river smells and leaf smoke and each other. Once they heard the mouse in the wall and Jay said some of her Wolfe piece, but the mouse didn't show himself.

"Clearly he's too modest."

"Clearly."

"You really did like the czarnina."

"I *loved* it."

"How can we improve on all this?"

She shrugged her shoulders, and Bill kissed them.

In the morning, as the first snow of the year fell, he delivered her to her apartment, then he went to work. He was sent back out with a photographer to cover a Halloween party at a grade school in Grosse Pointe. Driving on Jefferson Avenue they met two fire engines in full cry and followed them to the fringe of Bill's neighborhood.

The house was a two-story frame like every other crowded around the old glamour of Indian Village, and flames were licking up one side when they arrived, right behind the trucks. Benny, the photographer, scrambled out and started shooting. The house quickly filled with smoke and the firemen with axes, not eager to bust in, were visibly relieved when a teen-aged girl suddenly jumped from a second-floor window. She was kneeling in the snow, clutching a blanket to her stomach, when the captain ran over and demanded, "Is anyone else in there!" (Benny, fast behind the captain, was cursing his luck for being on the wrong side of the house and missing the jump.) She shook her head violently, crying, "My mama and daddy gone to work already!"

Apparently they had only walked over to Jefferson Avenue

to wait for a bus, because minutes later the mother came running up and embraced the girl, wailing, "My baby, my baby," followed by the father in coveralls, who threw his arms around them both and, hopping like a beefy tackle celebrating a touchdown, seemed to want to pick them up. But what he was really trying to do, it was soon clear, was get at the blanket his daughter had clutched to her stomach, and which he succeeded in doing only seconds before the captain barked, "Is this it, then!"

Veins and muscles bulged and twisted in the father's face, he was trying to answer and could not, and finally he charged toward the front door, one arm pointing, the other flopping as if broken, and his throat mercifully cleared. He screamed that her *boy* was still in there!

"I knew she had a kid," Benny grumbled. "They all do."

Two firemen, snapping on masks, disappeared through the door. The snow continued to fall. Everyone waited. The family huddled together and moaned and crooned Jesus' name, and Benny, on one knee, quietly crooning with them, shot them. Bill Rau looked down. He saw that he was standing on a newspaper with Cyrillic lettering. He wondered if some old Greek or Russian or Yugoslav or Bulgarian immigrant were there among them, or if only the wind blew the paper by.

"He got him! He got the kid!"

"Make way! Watch out!"

The fireman who brought out the boy handed him over, then coughing and swearing ripped his mask off, looking redfaced mad as hell and ready for a fight. They laid the boy in the snow. The captain shouted, "Get back! Get back now! Hold that woman back!"

"Baby, baby, stay back," the mother pleaded.

The father rested his big cheek on top of the girl's shoulder and appeared punch-drunk gazing at the blanket she clutched to her stomach, at the cream-colored feet now sticking out.

Benny kept his camera on her.

The whine of an ambulance came closer, but Bill Rau knew that the sounds around the boy were no good. The firemen worked on him hard until the ambulance arrived, but the sounds around him were hopeless. Cigarettes were lit. When the girl reached down and felt the doll she had rescued, when she brought it up and looked at it, her mouth stretched wide as if someone hateful were pulling at the corners, and Benny, kneeling in the snow, got the picture he wanted.

Bill Rau suddenly bolted from the picnic table, stumbling quickly away from it as if it might hurt him. Then he stopped and steadied himself. He was all right. "Yes, I'm all right," he said. Then jerking his head around, his expression confused, he said, "What?"

But no one sat at the table. No one had said anything.

A truck bearing a picture of a big loaf of bread groaned by. Bill watched the red taillights become smaller. When they disappeared his head seemed very light but workable. He fetched more bourbon for his glass.

Returning to the table he said, exuberantly, "By God!" He put a foot up on the table like a man in charge, like a man with a good story to tell. "By God!" he said again, and remembered.

They were married this very month, January. On an unseasonably warm, brilliant day for Detroit. Andy was best man and Louise Parrino, one of Jay's roommates, was maid of honor. Jay of course was beautiful, so beautiful that when Schooltz stepped aside to let Bill take her hand, Bill stepped aside with him—to allow her to move to wherever it was that such radiant women went, alone, to be even more beautiful. In fact she had to say his name twice before he finally took her hand. But he wasn't as nervous as people said. In his altar-boy days he had seen a groom or two roll up their eyeballs and go down like bundles of fancy rags for the Goodwill truck. But he was fine. He took Jay's hand and shook it as if they had just been introduced, yes (the photographer got this and it turned out to be Bill's favorite picture of the wedding), but when they knelt side by side waiting for the priest to begin, he most certainly did not say—as Andy claimed—"Hut sut rawlson on the rillerah with a brawla brawla sooit." People exaggerate.

Schooltz hosted lunch with champagne at the Belcrest (*his* in-laws, except for Great-aunt Liddy, drank grape juice; that lady, seated next to Mike Callahan, had several glasses of wine and then got a wicked fix on Mike's Vandyke, which she finally took hold of and refused to release until he gave her "a peck"), and afterwards, before Jay and Bill speeded off, Schooltz got Bill and his father in the men's room and produced a bottle of Wild Turkey and a glass.

"How many fingers?"

Then Bill's Polish uncles, sniffing out the action, came in and helped kill the bottle, toasting "Na zdrowie" and tossing down shots. Before Bill left the men's room another bottle had appeared and Schooltz was trying to say "Na zdrowie."

In the dining room Bill's mother and Helen and his aunts were trying, without much luck, to make conversation with Victoria, James, Regina, Richard, Mary, and Henry, who sat side by side in a half-circle and appeared, judging from their darting, magnified eyes, to be a little frightened. Or perhaps they were just worried about how to handle Great-aunt Liddy, who now had Eli the waiter by his lapel in a close monologue. Bill's grandmothers had Jay between them, dictating Polish and German recipes which Jay tried to record on napkins, and Mike and Phyl and other friends stood by finishing off the champagne and calling out ingredients she'd missed. They were all having a fine time with it.

When the newlyweds finally said good-bye, both Schooltz and Bill's mother cried, his mother saying she had *another one* in June, meaning Helen's wedding, and God knew if she would survive. "You!" she hugged Andy. "Don't you surprise me like these two!" Bill's father, uncomfortable around emotional displays, stood off to the side examining the old fretwork in the hotel's foyer, running his thumb over the beveled edges to see if they fit smoothly. "Two finish nails sticking up here—if I had my hammer I'd fix it for them," he said when Bill went to shake his hand. "Well, take it easy," they said in unison, and laughed, and Jay pinned a yellow rose beside Schooltz's carnation, and that was how the party ended.

Up north at the ski resort Jay learned how to snowplow on the beginner's hill, then wrote a certificate on a wedding napkin advancing herself to Intermediate. One night in their chalet Bill said, "I want to quit the paper."

"You should."

"I don't want to come home washed-out after writing who's and what's all day and feel sorry for myself and write about *that*."

"You shouldn't."

"Or more pages of bar-talk. I've got three hundred pages of bar-talk."

"Write about us! I mean, why not? And I'll go back to modeling full-time and you can have all day—"

"No. I'll get a teaching job like Mike's. You want to fondle more Jucits? What fun is that? Look—"

Their bed was in a loft, which overlooked the fireplace. Every night, no matter how much chatter they made under the quilt, a field mouse by and by gathered himself before the hearth.

"What do you suppose he thinks about?" Jay whispered.

"Bacon."

"We should feed him."

"No, Francis Bacon. And chicken."

"What are you talking about?"

"I am talking about why you will never catch that learned mouse stuffing a chicken full of snow."

"Stop it. Why not?"

"Because that's how the great scientist caught a chill and passed to his reward. What?"

"I didn't say anything."

"You said I should write about us."

"Yes."

"Give me ten good reasons."

"Because we're happy."

"'Her feet beneath her petticoat, / Like little mice, stole in and out, / As if they feared the light; / But oh, she dances such a way, / No sun upon an Easter day / Is half so fine a sight.' Sir John Suckling. 'A Ballad Upon a Wedding.'"

"We should dance, Billy."

"Why, I think we are."

*

Back in Detroit Bill wrote to several colleges inquiring about openings in their English departments. In February Jay was pregnant, and six weeks later miscarried. In June at Helen's wedding reception in Bill's parents' back yard, she took his arm and whispered she needed to lie down for a while. "I just think it's the wine." He helped her to his old bed. "I'm fine, Billy. Really." Checking on her later he found her on the bathroom floor. "Please don't come in." But he already saw what she didn't want him to see. He flushed the toilet and drove her to the hospital.

When the doctor let him see her, she cried, "Something's wrong with me, Billy. Something *is*."

"Are you kidding? Do you know how many miscarriages my aunt Nellie had before those strapping thugs she calls her sons started coming out?"

Jay rolled her head on the pillow. She'd been given a sedative.

"Guess," said Bill.

"Two?"

"Four!"

"Did she really?"

"And this doctor told me what what's-his-name in Detroit said, that miscarriages are common as the common cold, practically."

"He just told me they're not unusual."

She was drifting off. "Billy? You don't have to tell them, your mother and the others, do you?" But she was under before he could tell her not to worry about it.

In early August, when they had about given up, a college in the Upper Peninsula offered Bill a job. They were off, first to the Callahan's cottage, where they swam and browned and stayed up late over long, jolly, exotic dinners, and where Jay got back her confidence, and then to the U.P. They took a faculty apartment, walked under the brilliant reds and yellows of the hardwood forests nearby, and Jay enrolled for a full load of classes. She also found a pediatrician she liked. "It doesn't hurt to have one," she said, "just in case." In late October she became pregnant again, and miscarried the week before Christmas.

At first she seemed to take it calmly, believing, as the doctor insisted, that these things happen. But on New Year's Eve while dressing to go out for dinner, she suddenly threw herself on the bed and cried over and over that she was no good. The doctor had prescribed hormones and stimulants and other drugs to help her conceive and carry the fetus—but nothing would work! she sobbed. Not ever! "I'm rotten inside, Billy, I'm rotten and sick and I won't ever have a baby!"

When they first arrived in Marquette they were told the standard weather joke up there—that the U.P. had two seasons: ten months of winter and two months of poor sledding. Now it was less of a joke. The spectacular autumn they'd had was a fluke or even a trick. The ice on the lake moved toward shore and piled up in places a story high, jagged and poked through with pieces of timber; and the ice was gray—the color of the sky, of the days, of people's eyes. Almost every evening, it seemed the local paper carried a short notice of a death that, when not officially declared as such, was likely a suicide. The rate was high. A lot of old miners on relief sat in bars all day and brooded. It was a depressed area, people kept saying. They were too far from anything, any city, that could offer diversion, people kept saying. They were stuck with themselves! Even the little faculty parties were depressing—especially for Jay—because several wives were pregnant or had recently had babies. And when an invitation to a quilting or a shower arrived, Jay would have the blues for days. Bill had them with her. He was not writing anything that amounted to much.

In February he signed up to teach an extension course at the SAC base nearby, for summer money. As soon as the school year ended, he and Jay were getting the hell away from there—downstate to the Callahan's cottage! Upper Minnesota was not much fun for Mike and Phyl, either. Though they could write goofy letters about a favorite pipe in their trailer freezing or bursting again, and though Mike's descriptions of trying to fix anything could make Jay suddenly laugh, their letters finally were only a reminder of the long northern gloom in which nearly everyone seemed to have the blues. Except that the Callahans also had Sunny and Kate. A fact which neither Bill nor Jay needed to mention.

He did not enjoy teaching at the SAC base. He had fifteen students in the class—pilots, navigators, and two officers' wives. When they read Thoreau and Emerson and Dickinson, Bill sometimes wondered why. Vietnam was looking worse—everything was looking worse. But often what made him feel pointless, the *words* pointless, came down to the pistols the men wore at their hips.

In contrast to their uniforms, the pistols were personal. Some were ivory-handled, some black-handled, one even had a red handle; and all, it seemed, had a name scratched into them—the owner's, a girlfriend's, a wife's. "Why do you guys carry those things?" Bill asked a navigator once, during their coffee break. "In case there's a mutiny," the navigator said, "or in case things look real bad." He had a Ph.D. in math and was counting the days he had left to serve. Both pieces of information—about the pistols and about his eagerness to get out—had been given casually, in the same way he might ask someone to pass the sugar. And he was not the only man in class who spoke as if words were without weight, clash, music, and all the rest.

Bill could not find a way to tell the students that Emily Dickinson loved words, was made to tremble by them. They seemed satisfied to read her poems for their simplest, crudest messages, and to agree with her that death is a mystery, that failures rank success high. As for Emerson and Thoreau, they were dreamers. Two or three members of the class said they probably would be taken for Communists today, and their works therefore would not be as popular with some teachers. The wives in the class felt sorry for Thoreau and for his brother John because Ellen Sewall refused them both.

Like the navigator Bill counted the time left. And tried not to think too hard about those men sitting before him in their bulky On Alert gear, who were prepared to shoot themselves with their pistols, if necessary. And if the deafening Alert buzzer interrupted class, as it did often during the quarter, reducing their number usually to the two wives and to Bill, he would feel that "school"—the school they were playing—was over for the night, and go home.

Spring came, officially, and looked no different than the season before. Lake Superior lay in its large gray skin. A local dentist took a shotgun into his office one morning and shot up his furniture. But Jay was feeling better. She had a history class she liked. And then one day Bill stood in the doorway and opened his coat, showing her a puppy under his arm. Jay squealed and clapped and hopped up and down until Bill whispered, "The regulations!" Only fish and birds were allowed in the faculty apartments.

Maude was a German shepherd runt, barely four weeks old. She came from Hennessey, a student of Bill's who worked part-time at the kennel that supplied guard dogs for the air base. Showing signs of hip dysplasia, and a runt besides, she would have been destroyed. The Raus declared April Fool's Day her birthday. Hiding her from the Maintenance people, they were like poachers on the czar's estate who had captured his prize roe, Jay said. She also said, fiercely, "No one's going to eat *you*, little Maude."

Because the dog had been weaned too soon, she did not know how to take her milk or any other food. Jay taught her, mothered her, and promptly dismissed two vets as "cold" before she found one sensitive enough to advise her. She cut classes when Bill could not be home to watch Maude. When Bill did watch the dog, he had a detailed list of instructions to guide him.

At last the tentative drips of a thaw arrived. People smiled sheepishly at the sun as at an old friend who hadn't betrayed them after all. The Raus took Maude for short walks in the sun, Jay selecting the area, the very ground, as carefully as if she were shopping for a fine fabric. "We don't want her to catch cold or come down with colic," she'd say with utter seriousness. She carried a towel for when Maude ran through a puddle or under a wet bush. In the car she kept a wool blanket—Maude's blanket—that she insisted Maude wear wrapped around her for the ride home. When the dog was about ten weeks old, getting stronger by the day and clearly annoyed at the towel and blanket rituals, Jay laughed, "I guess I *have* been a little fussy."

Real signs of spring worked their sweet magic on Jay. The Raus no longer had to avoid references to the miscarriages; and she could say to Bill with casual confidence, "When we have our baby, Mr. Rau, I intend to breastfeed it. Even if it's twins."

Or, playfully, "I've been thinking how grand you'd look in a beard, Billy. I mean look at Nicholas, here," she was reading her history text beside him in bed. "There's a resemblance, wouldn't you say? In the face? And think of all the children he sired."

A few nights later, however, when Maude's barking woke him and he looked over to see if Jay had also been disturbed by it, he saw that her cheeks were glistening wet with tears. He wondered how many other nights she wept in her sleep, and in what shapes her fears came to her then, and what would happen if their luck did not change.

Around that time Bill had a recurring dream which spoke to his own unrest:

He was in church, in a pew near the front, waiting for Jay to appear in her wedding dress. Over at the side, a priest sat in the confessional box, looking out a little window at the congregation. At the rear of the church several people were gathered for the walk down the center aisle. Their faces were a blur to Bill and he felt lousy for having ruined the pre-dance party. For having backed the blue-haired housemother against the wall barking Marx at her, and for being drunk and heaving his guts all over the stainless steel sink in the sorority kitchen, embarrassing Annie in front of her sisters.

Now, for punishment, he couldn't come to the reception.

The priest in the confessional box had nothing more to say. He looked at Bill with a green, grainy face—a face from an old TV screen. "Are you Italian?" Bill asked him. But the green face had no more to say. Maybe because, Bill thought, he needed a shave . . . or because his red tuxedo was not appropriate in the house of God.

"But I came straight from the dance," he explained, "and all I have is this shoe horn." Glancing back at the wedding party to see how much time he had, Bill began quickly to scrape his cheek with the shoe horn.

Several of Annie's sorority sisters held her long train as she walked down the aisle. She stopped at Bill's pew, but kept her eyes straight ahead and said, "Promise me, Billy. Promise me you won't talk about politics in front of my friends anymore." She was keeping her eyes straight ahead, smiling the smile in her group sorority picture for the photographer who was waiting at the altar. The acolytes, meanwhile, were draping a white sheet over a casket, and the pastor was saying:

"And so, just as Christ's death was joyful, not sorrowful, just as a blanket of snow means fresh water for the farmer's fields come spring—so too this white sheet, this mantle of purity. And now, let us join hands. Let us lift our hearts to Him who dies and dies, knowing He will see our loved one home."

Bill's cheeks were clean-shaven now, but the shoe horn was not sharp enough to cut the extra putty off his chin . . .

He would waken from the dream and get out of bed and smoke a cigarette at the table that held his typewriter and pencils and foundering novel. He would smoke and write his dream in the dark, and the next day throw it away.

At last the school year was over! Before they loaded the car for the trip downstate, they moved their possessions to an apartment that Hennessey and his wife Thelma were vacating later that summer. It was closer to town and took up the entire second floor of a large old storybook house with turrets and towers and caryatids and canopies. The house was owned by an eccentric named Brown and his sister Violet, who lived on the first floor with Brown's dog Spooker Brown.

"He looks like Louis the Eleventh, also known as 'The Universal Spider,'" Jay said, meaning Brown, meaning his walnut walking stick and baggy clothes and the grand way he waved good-bye to them from his high-backed chair on the porch of his castle-like house. And later she would find more in the eccentric to liken to that monarch. But first there was the summer, *the* summer.

At his picnic table at the edge of the desert Bill Rau raised his glass to the stars. "By God, yes," he said. He slapped his thigh, smiling.

When they got to the Mackinac Bridge after four hours of driving past what seemed nothing but stunted jack pine followed by stunted jack pine (how beautiful that country had looked to them last September), they whooped and sang their way across, and then immediately stopped on the other side at a flag-draped Mackinaw City tourist shop filled with fake Ojibway and Ottawa and Huron souvenirs—never mind, they were back in the Lower Peninsula!—and bought ice cream cones for themselves and a Dixie Cup for Maude. Then they picked up Highway 31 and drove through Petoskey and Charlevoix and Traverse City and Manistee and on down the western side of the state past the cherry orchards and apple orchards and blueberry fields to the Callahan's place where Bill tooted the horn under their giant beech bringing them forth, glasses in hand, to usher them up to the cottage just in time to see the sun roar welcome before it slipped brazenly into Lake Michigan. After which Bill and Jay found a second wind and talked and laughed with the Callahans until dawn.

Except for a visit to Bill's family and one to Pontiac to see Schooltz and Victoria, James, Regina, Richard, Mary, and Henry, they stayed at the Callahan's through Labor Day. They came back from Flint loaded down with jars of his mother's tomato juice and jellies, and back from Pontiac with the news that Schooltz had met a widow from Houghton Lake. Her name was Mabel. She was sort of in the real estate business, he said, which was how he met her, looking for a little place up north near the fishing for when he retired from the factory in the fall. Jay couldn't get any more information out of him. In fact the Raus heard no more about Schooltz and Mabel until they received a Polaroid picture of the two of them grinning (he shyly, carnationed) in front of the stone fireplace in her cottage, with his chicken-scratch message on the back: "Meet the Mr. and Mrs.!" That was in October, when Jay was four months pregnant and doing fine.

The U.P. was like another country for them now. The autumn colors were brilliant and sassy as last year, but this time seemed to last weeks longer, and walking among them Jay blushed deeper and redder than the richest oak or maple they could find. Mornings when the sun filled the little round turret room where she kept her books and sewing basket, Bill would find her there in her robe rocking and softly humming, one hand holding her brush like a wand, the other down on Maude's back idly making curlicues in her hair. If she feared that this pregnancy too would collapse, she did not show it. Much of the time she seemed on the periphery of a world in which knights and their ladies took long afternoon lunches on a quilt on the green, or sat on a large outcropping of rock by the ocean looking for the King's fleet to return with new spices; a world in which Brown's storybook house was a proper place to live.

And thus they lived there, Presque Isle Park nearby their green and Lake Superior, ample with rock perches, their ocean. And Maude their pet deer. "Does all this sound like a prime-fed cliché!" Bill Rau demanded of the desert stars. Well if it does, he thought, it wasn't then. Then it was, as Jay said, simply the life they had been waiting for. Add to it old Spooker Brown shaking off the frost in his stiffened bones, head held high and back legs scratching the dirt, to take on all the hot-loined young bucks that came sniffing into the yard after Maude in her first heat. Add to it the amaryllis and oxalis and coleus and geraniums and African violets and all the other plants she collected and had hanging from every window in the apartment and which bloomed on even the grayest days. Add to it the night they walked out to the end of an ore dock and there, at the edge, four or five stories above Lake Superior's moon-slickened surface, picked the name Jenny, certain they would have a girl. Add to it the New Year's Eve in the Northland Hotel, dancing, and Jay guiding his hand to the kicking place. Add to it even events that happened years later, the Hotel At-lantico in Cadiz, for example, when all the lights suddenly went out and he lit matches for Jay to help Jenny from the tub and into her clothes and then Jenny, opening the door and seeing people in the hall with candles, yelling, "They're coming to rescue us!" But do not add the figure down on the ground on all fours under the desert stars, retching, trying to bring up more, and producing only the head-shake of a trucker who happened to catch a glimpse of the figure in passing.

Part Two

4

Everything seemed very clear. The fire, the hospital, the doctor, even the business with Richer the mortician. Jay's outburst and fainting were also clear. And it made perfect sense to me when the doctor suggested she stay that first night in the hospital. But she wouldn't listen to him. Then Leah Robinson, who lived across the street, tried to get us to go back to her house. My God, didn't she realize we'd have to see our house?

Leah finally understood and drove us to the Hotel Fort Des Moines. "Since it is Christmas," I said, "the liquor stores will be closed." She understood that too and went home and brought us a full bottle. She offered to call our relatives. I said I would. But I didn't call anyone.

Up in the room I found a long piece of string. To pass the time I tied it, slowly, into many small knots. To pass more time, I went out and walked a lot. Jay usually came with me.

Then on the Thursday after Christmas we walked to the funeral home, a minister read a few words, and they cremated Jenny. That afternoon at the Greyhound terminal on Keosauqua I bought a ticket for Mexico.

I got as far as the edge of the desert. I drank whiskey at a picnic table between my motel and the highway until I passed out. When someone slapped me awake I stuck out my thumb. A guy in a van took me all the way to Denver. His name was Poppy.

"It used to be something else," he said, "but all the used-to-be's are back *there,* you follow me? From D. D. Eisenhower to Tricky, including all the wooden fish with numbers on them you paid a quarter at the carnival to scoop out with a net in between, you follow me? I mean, I caught the winning TD on the last play of the last game of my senior year in high school and Ike was *still* in office. And married the prettiest, richest, most spoiled lady in town the next year, under handsome Jack. We were nineteen and had *all* of our dream furniture, baby. You follow me? During the week I traveled my territory, the entire state, selling high school yearbooks. On weekends I came home to my stuffed prize from the top shelf. Some guys understand, some don't (I myself chuckle over it now if I'm in the right mood), but what drove me *out* was her God damn belching. I mean she brought up these great froggy blasts from her toejam, man, and turned them into words, like a cancer-croaker. In bed, you follow me?

"I split. My father-in-law tried to get me drafted but I hot-wired cars and ran red lights until they caught me and gave me a little time. He was satisfied, I was satisfied. Then after handsome Jack went down, I fell in with a chick who was socially conscious. Did the whole number with her. I mean I *liked* it, made me feel good marching and running the mimeograph machine, staying up all night smoking a lot of cigarettes planning our next move. We shall overcome, right? I'll tell you how much I liked it. The chick was creamy, an ice cream cone, va-nilla, man, and *all* that time, about two years, I never balled her once. Not that I didn't try, you understand. But two years, man, is a long time to be more or less faithful to the same chick without balling her. She was a real believer, you follow me?"

There was more to his story—a commune, a bar he started, some dealing, one or two other business ventures, but I kept nodding off (his dope, my lack of sleep) and finally I slept awhile. When I heard him again he talked about running a novelty shop with "a fine lady" who made most of the jewelry.

"I'll tell you how I got my name Poppy, man, it's a nice thing. My lady's kid called me that the first time he saw me. I mean I'd just met her, and pretty soon we see we want to jimmy a little, you know, so she invites me over. She's got a kid, wow. Like I thought she was maybe sixteen, and here's this two-year-old boy sacked on the couch. It turns out she *is* only sixteen, but that's another story. The point is, she shows me this fantastic jewelry she's made out of *nothing*—pennies, washers—and before we ball or anything I say, 'We gotta go into business!' Next morning the kid sees me and says, 'Poppy!' I say, 'Right, man, that's me,' just playing along. But—and here's the good part—when Fizzy and me start the business and it takes off, man, I *remembered* when it all started, you follow me? I mean I believe in *signs*. So I changed my name, legally. And guess what we're gonna call our new store? Poppy's Place!"

It was about ten o'clock in the morning when he dropped me off at the bus station in Denver.

"What day is it?"

"Monday, man. Wash day." Pulling away he flashed me the peace sign, smiling, and I saw he had a gold eyetooth.

I felt weak. Inside the station I sat down. For a long time I waited for my body to stop trembling, feeling old, wanting a bowl of hot soup. Steaming, nourishing bowls of chicken noodle, tomato, onion, mushroom came to me but I couldn't reach them. I sat up straight, like a good boy, but I couldn't get out of the chair. The bowls of hot soup came to me one by one, each with a big silver spoon, and disappeared, untouched.

Finally I was up, outside. The sky was high and skull white. I found a restaurant, got down chili and coffee, then I found a hotel and slept until the next morning, when I boarded a bus for Des Moines.

I knew what I'd done to Jay and felt weak all over again. I knew it before I climbed in Poppy's van; knew it probably even as I was leaving the funeral home; and now in that droning bus I kept seeing a vision of myself as a child's stick-figure drawing with a balloon-shaped head trying to leap off the writing tablet in a jerky silent-movie motion, but whenever I reached the edge of the paper, there was another sheet I had to run across and try to escape, followed by yet another, until I put my head in my bag somewhere in the middle of those gray flat fields of snow in the middle of Nebraska and vomited.

When we stopped for a few minutes in Ogallala I got some change and called her office. A woman answered.

"Is Mrs. Rau there?"

"I'm sorry, I don't know," she said. "Everyone's up in the coffee room. It's somebody's birthday or something."

"Who are you?"

"I don't work here. I'm just looking for an earring."

In North Platte I tried again and got a janitor. "I shooed them all out," he said, "so I can wax the floor."

"Can you tell me if she's still in the building? Near another phone? Can you switch me to somebody else?"

"Oh boy, these buttons always mess me up. Why don't you call upstairs to the main secretary?"

I asked him for that number. He wheezed into the phone,

looking it up; when he finally got it I had to go. At the next stop, Kearney, it was six o'clock and too late to reach her at the office. I bought a candy bar at a vending machine. Why hadn't I taken a plane in Denver? I turned to a woman holding a baby and said, "I have three credit cards in my wallet." She smiled; a front tooth was missing. "I'm sorry," I said. "I'm just tired."

"So's Melissa. And her pants is wet."

In Omaha—an hour's layover—I washed my face, threw out the vomit-covered shirt in my bag, changed some bills. Her boss, if anyone, would know where she was. I got his number at home.

"Jay resigned," he told me. "I tried to talk her into taking a leave but . . . well, I understood." He said deepest sympathies, etc., and I was trying to understand how I could have thought she would go back to work.

"Where can I reach her? I . . ."

"She gave us her dad's address in Michigan."

I called Schooltz's number in Houghton Lake. No answer. It was after midnight. Where could they be on a Tuesday night? Playing cards? They played a lot of cards. Jay too? But she didn't have to be in Houghton Lake—she just gave that address. Where was she, then? I tried the number again. Nothing. My bus was called. Still nothing. But I was unable to move. I watched the janitors mop, the drunks slide in and out, red- and yellow-eyed, and dialed Schooltz's number. At five o'clock I walked around outside, stepping on cracks breaking backs, and took a cab to the airport.

In Des Moines I called Leah Robinson, some other friends. No, no one had heard from her, though Leah did say she'd seen her in the hotel the day after the funeral.

"Did she say anything? I mean about her plans?"

"She was waiting for you, Billy."

"Was she OK, was she all right?"

Leah started to cry and I hung up.

I couldn't believe she'd still be there, but I called the Fort Des Moines anyway and learned she'd checked out on January 3, leaving no messages. She'd waited there five days for me. I tried Schooltz; still nothing. I went to the bank, then to the post office and picked up magazines, Christmas cards, bills, but nothing from her. Did I expect a letter? Dear Billy, here I sit . . . Five days in that box of a room.

She was waiting for you, Billy. On the flight to Chicago I saw myself in front of a door, the door to her apartment, almost sixteen years ago . . . it looked just like a door in a hotel . . . she wore a white dress, her cheeks were flushed, we were going to her roommate's wedding . . . Then I opened the door again, the hotel's door, that room, after the funeral, and said I had to go out for a while. She sat on the bed and looked at me and said nothing. Not where are you going, nothing. And if she had asked I could not have told her, though I did know I'd need money. I went to the bank. I remembered doing that. Then the bus station . . . arriving in Kansas City and buying a shirt and a duffel bag, because my turtleneck was wet and because I knew I'd be checking into a hotel sooner or later and ought to have a bag. And I remembered before that, before the funeral, walking past what was left of our house, knowing while I was doing it that I had never wanted to see that house again, and yet there I was, looking at the boarded-up windows, the caved-in roof, and then walking around back and seeing the angels in the snow. They were still there, though nobody but me would have recognized them because of all the footprints . . .

At O'Hare, after we landed, it was a while before we could get to the terminal: they'd had a record snowfall, the captain said, and everything was behind schedule. The stewardess came by taking drink orders. I didn't want a drink. I wanted to move! Inside, finally, I kept trying Schooltz's number and heard only the same cricket-like signal, which was now staying in my head between calls. Where could they *be*? In the corridor people were walking past me in a hurry, back and forth, up the corridor and down, carrying sacks and bags, suits and fruit and babies, in wingtips, loafers, high heels, wooden clogs, mukluks, cowboy boots, sandals, sneakers, galoshes, on slim ankles, on thick, on flat feet, dragging a foot, dragging a child, all going up the corridor or down, which was what they were supposed to do, it was their job, their pastime, their passion, their burden, their nervous tic. And mine too once I left the phone and joined them.

Crickkk-ettt . . . crickkk-ettt . . .

I asked the operator to try for me, to check the line, maybe something was wrong with the connection. No, she said, everything seemed to be all right. Then I thought, Carl and Eunice in the brown house stayed up there year-round, he even kept Schooltz's driveway plowed, what was their last name! Carl and Eunice, Carl and Eunice . . . but no last name came to me. Their other neighbors, their card-playing friends . . . Frank and Melba, Connie and Leonard . . . or Frank and Connie, Leonard and Melba. They were all just pairs of first names.

The only people whose last names I could think of were our old neighbors, Ellen Shipley and the Hanks, but they were not there in the winter.

Pinky! He'd know if Schooltz was around. It was a Mobil station on North Shore Road, I told the operator, Pinky's Mobil or North Shore Mobil, something like that, or Pinky's Baits.

"I show a Martin's Mobil on North Shore," she said, and I got the number. A man answered.

"Pinky?"

"That's me."

"Pinky, this is Schooltz's son-in-law, Bill Rau, I'm trying to reach him at home and nobody answers, have you seen him or Mabel around?"

"Say, is this long-distance? I can hear it buzz to Christmas."

"Yes, have you seen them?"

"Not today, or yesterday either, but he's around, they both are. Least they haven't asked me to check on their furnace like they do when they go away. Unless they asked Carl up the road, but I don't think so since his heart attack, you know."

"So you saw Schooltz when, couple days ago?"

"Couple days ago, Monday. Filled up the Olds. Where you calling from—that's some buzz, ain't it?"

"Chicago, I'm on my way over."

"Well, they'll be glad to hear that. Say, I see you sold your place to some fella from Saginaw, Mabel says. Hear he's gonna cut down all them nice trees and build."

"If you see Schooltz, Pinky, tell him I'm coming, will you?"

"Sure will."

"Wait. You haven't seen, I mean my wife went on ahead of me a few days ago . . . I wonder if she got there yet."

"Haven't seen her."

It was one o'clock. My plane left at two. I'd land in Midland a little after three, rent a car, and be at Schooltz's right around sunset. OK, I thought, OK, OK, and started to walk. I was excited. I hadn't reached Schooltz or Mabel, but I'd talked to Pinky Martin, bait man and furnace watcher, and considered that the next best thing, plus something of a good sign. At the concession I bought a sandwich and milk, but ate too fast and my stomach bunched like a fist. I smoked a cigarette, trying to relax, trying not to think where she might be—because if she wasn't in Des Moines or Houghton Lake, where was she!

Schooltz and Mabel would know. Really the problem was not that difficult. She'd left Schooltz's address at her office, now it was simply a matter of reaching Schooltz. She was probably with them at that moment.

But if she was, why hadn't Pinky Martin seen her? She'd left the Fort Des Moines a week ago, surely he would've seen or heard something of her around the lake in a week's time? If she flew straight to Michigan—if she even *went* to Michigan. Was she still in Des Moines? If so, where? I called all of our friends. Did she check into another hotel, not able to stand the Fort Des Moines any longer? If she did that, why no message for me at the desk?

Suddenly my face felt hot. Maybe she didn't want me to know where she was? Maybe she went back to the politician's lackey?

I heard my flight being called. I'd try Schooltz's number once more. All the phones near my boarding area were in use, eight men in dark suits with vests. Finally I found one free. A busy signal! They were home! Or I'd poked a wrong number. I tried again, slowly, and again the busy signal. It was almost like reaching someone. But now I had to catch my plane.

We sat on the runway for nearly an hour, waiting our turn. I tried to read a magazine, but the thought of Jay going back to the lackey kept getting in the way. His concern, she said, for the Russian dissidents in labor camps . . . his marriage falling apart . . . Why didn't she just go upstairs, use our bedroom, when she had the chance? I asked her. She didn't want to use our bed, she said. Did we really say those things? Was her lover really a Ph.D. who ran a mimeograph machine, licked stamps, for a state legislator?

I lay back and traced "No Smoking" on the roof of my mouth with my tongue, over and over, until I saw Jay in Michigan, at the cottage, racing me out to the dock for our morning swim. We bought the cottage—Realtor Mabel's "find" for us— the summer Jay was promoted to editor of *Midwest Politics*. The same summer my first book came out and Jenny graduated from nursery school. We'd been in Iowa three years then, and having a place in Michigan, if only for vacations, was like coming home. Jenny turned the fishing shanty into her playhouse, and at night, at the end of the dock, we could see *stars*. Most nights when just the three of us were there, we skinny-dipped, Jay and I, and afterwards sat on the dock in our robes and drank a brandy, facing north, recalling the Upper Peninsula and searching the sky for the star that lay brightest above the silo our last year up there, Jenny's first, when we lived an easy walk from Lake Superior. "It's *that* star," she'd finally decide, bringing our past forward, locating one more time a part that stood for many, all of them as romantic and private and fragile as the things we can do only once, and which we preserve in a single gesture or sign that others would consider ordinary or corny unless it was their gesture or sign too. I thought of Poppy then, his faith in signs and his verb "to jimmy."

Shortly before we landed I fell into a squeezed, deep sleep and dreamt an old dream in which I was wearing a red tuxedo and trying to scrape putty off my chin with a shoe horn.

It was after four when I entered the Midland terminal. First I called Schooltz—no answer—then rented a car and discovered, as the Hertz woman warned, that the interstate was icy. The car would suddenly slide two or three feet to the side. I cut my speed from seventy to fifty, concentrating hard on the road. It was getting dark fast and my eyes started to burn. Also, after a violent lurch moved me completely into the next lane, my hands and arms began to tremble. I needed coffee. I'd been up and traveling since Denver, forty hours ago. How many miles was that? And all the miles before Denver? I couldn't think about that now. I opened the window, turned off the heat, and repeated the alphabet until I shivered.

At a rest stop north of Clare I put my face in a sink of cold water, tried Schooltz again, drank a cup of machine coffee and took another cup back to the car. It was pitch dark now. Every ten minutes or so a van or pickup hauling a pair of snowmobiles passed me, and across the divide traffic was slim too. People were home eating, that's where they were. Eating and watching TV in their socks, or over at the Elks for the Wednesday night fish fry and bingo game. It started to sleet. I kept the speedometer steady at fifty, which would get me to Schooltz's around eight. If I didn't hit a deer. I remembered the summer night after I graduated from college, driving up north in the '46 Chevy I'd paid a hundred dollars for, to see Annie at the place near Charlevoix her parents had rented. East of Mancelona, in the dusk, a doe bounded out. She was just a little thing, carrying probably her first fawn. I broke her neck, and my front end was smashed in, steaming. I had a bloody nose. Someone finally came along and gave me a lift into Mancelona, where I called the Conservation office, sold the car for junk, and stuck out my thumb. Next day while her parents played golf, Annie and I lay in the cottage and were careful, careful.

I pulled into Schooltz's at ten past eight. No one was home, though his driveway was cleared and the back door unlocked. I looked for signs that Jay had been there and found nothing—the beds were all made, the fireplace swept, the *National Geographic*s and *Reader's Digest*s neatly stacked on the coffee table. What did I expect to find! Everything we owned had burned. Then I remembered Leah giving Jay a purple comb, and I went back through all the rooms. No purple comb, no extra toothbrush, no dirty underwear that wouldn't fit Mabel. My mouth felt like flannel. I went to the kitchen again, for a drink of water, and saw in the sink a small glass with a ring of milk at the bottom. I got some milk on my finger and tasted it. It was fresh.

The phone rang, almost knocking the glass out of my hand.

"Hello?" It was a woman's voice.

"This is Bill Rau."

"Well, this is Eunice next door and I just called to see if Mabel left a note about where they are."

"No, where are they?"

"Well, they stayed in Cadillac last night. She was seeing about some property and because of the storm that hit west of here, and pretty bad too, I hear, they decided not to take a chance. When she called me she thought they'd try to be back tonight, but if not to check on the furnace. You folks find it working OK? Carl looked in this morning after clearing the drive, because we got some of that storm ourselves, and more now by the looks of it, and said it was on."

"I just got here. The house is warm, it must be on."

"You just got there?"

"About fifteen minutes ago."

"Well your wife must've come ahead then."

"What do you mean?"

"She was there this afternoon."

"Are you *sure?*"

"Well . . . yes." She sounded insulted. "We even waved."

"When was that? What time?"

"Well . . . it had to be around two because the mail'd just come and Carl and me was leaving for town. Just a minute, I'll ask him to make sure."

"No, no, that's all right."

"Carl," I heard her say, "it's Schooltz's son-in-law, he wants to know what time it was when we saw his wife in the yard, remember? Around two when Alfred come by, wasn't it?" To me, "Carl says right after the mail truck come by, around two. We thought you was all together."

"You saw somebody with her?"

"Well, no. We just thought you'd all come in the same car like always. It had Iowa plates and, well, we figured you and your daughter was in the house."

"What was she doing when you saw her?"

"Oh . . . just in the yard, standing there. Unpacking the car, I think. Is something wrong?"

"I don't know. She did come on ahead of me, but now I don't know where she is."

"Well, the car was gone and nobody answered the phone when we come back from town, about five, because I said to Carl, 'I should've told her about Schooltz and Mabel being in Cadillac, in case they didn't leave a note.' The house was dark but I called anyway thinking maybe one of you had gone to town and the others stayed home to watch TV, but like I say nobody answered, which now naturally I understand why. Then when I see the lights I called again and you answered. Well, my goodness, where would she be, d'you suppose? On a night like this?"

I thanked her and hung up. She thought Jay was unpacking the car. Like a robot I checked all the rooms and closets again. But what was I looking for!

It was almost nine and sleet was clicking on the front windows. Beyond them, the lake was a plain of darkness; the darker shapes here and there were fishing shanties. I couldn't even make out the beginning of a treeline. Lake, timber, and sky were all the same—an emptiness spitting sleet toward me. I turned on the yard light and the sleet bloomed into the shaggy end of a monstrous gray beard being whipped by the wind.

Where *would* she go in this weather! We had no friends up there that time of year, she wouldn't call on Schooltz and Mabel's friends (Eunice didn't even suggest that possibility), there was food in the house—

The cottage. And likely it was empty: Mabel had said the Saginaw man bought it strictly as an investment. And unless he changed the locks, which I doubted, she'd find the extra key Jenny always kept in the shanty.

The ice on the road was worse, but county trucks were out flashing their yellow lights and throwing sand. My armpits were wet. The cottage was just two miles away. I marked off the first bridge, the Wolcjacks' jig-sawed black bear cubs with their names, Steve and Bea, written out in reflectors on the bears' bellies, the three white pines where Ellen, the former teacher, worked at her watercolors, the second bridge, the fussy pharmacist's spread protected by his Cyclone fence and dogs, the long curve skirting the cedar marsh, then straight ahead on the right our tallest Norway. But what I wanted to see was a car with Iowa plates parked beside the road, and I didn't. And nothing sat in the long driveway but weeks of snow. And the house was dark.

I got out of my car anyway—I didn't know what else to do—and looked at the snowmobile tracks and boot tracks that my lights picked up along the ridge of snow on the shoulder. It looked like several snowmobilers had rendezvoused there and got off their machines. Then I saw fresher tracks, leading to or from the house, I couldn't be sure. Angling the car so that my lights showed more of the yard, I followed the tracks in.

The snow was deep—up past my knees in the drifts. I followed the tracks to the back door, then around to the front where a chest-high drift lay the length of the house, close in; but whoever it was didn't attempt that drift to get to the door, instead headed straight for the shanty at the edge of the yard. I could feel my heartbeat. They had to be her tracks—and she remembered the key. I reached the back door again. Locked.

With a piece of oak off the woodpile I busted the glass in both the storm and inner doors.

Everything inside was shut off for the winter. But someone had had a fire in there recently, I could smell it. I lit a match and went over to the fireplace and found a candle. When the flame filled out it wasn't even necessary to look in the grate. On the hearth I saw a cluster of orange peels and Jenny's key beside them.

When I got back to Schooltz's they were there, at the door, both talking at once. I walked past them into the kitchen and picked up the phone. They stopped talking. "Dial Eunice's number for me," I said to Mabel. When Eunice answered I asked for a description of Jay's car. "Oh dear . . . light-colored, white, I think, or maybe cream. Let me ask Carl." I waited. "He says a white Ford Fairlane, a '78." Then I called the state police and reported her missing—something I should have done two hours ago. Then I sat down.

"Can I have a drink, Schooltz?"

He got out a bottle and glass and Mabel twisted a Kleenex. After a couple of swallows I repeated some of the information I'd given the police: "She's been gone from here since at least five o'clock—probably two or three hours before that. Where, Schooltz? Where?"

"And where is that *child?*" Mabel said.

The phone rang and I leaped for it. It was Eunice wondering if she and Carl could do anything. Yes, I said, don't call us anymore, we wanted the line free. I lit a cigarette. "In the last two weeks," I said, "has she written or called?"

Mabel shook her head in small jerks, ready to cry. "We haven't heard anything," Schooltz said, "since her card."

"What card?"

"Christmas card," Mabel said. "With the magazine subscriptions. We called to thank you for them and wish you . . ." She stopped, unable to continue, and Schooltz said, "We called Christmas morning and talked to Jenny. She said you was out on the golf course, skiing . . . and she was making a surprise breakfast."

"Is she missing too?" Mabel waited for the worst.

"No."

"Well where *is* she?"

"In Iowa," I said and swallowed more whiskey. Then I went over to the sink and splashed water on my face. None of us said anything for a while. I watched the sleet come down. Schooltz poured himself a drink and rubbed the stubs on his three-fingered hand. Mabel twisted her Kleenex.

I'd taken a trip after Christmas, I told them, and this morning, when I got back to Des Moines, Jay wasn't there. "I don't know when she left, but she came here . . . apparently drove all the way."

Mabel went over to the TV set and returned with one of the Christmas cards that had been displayed on it.

"See, here's her card."

"And we already got one of the magazines," Schooltz added. "Didn't we, Mabel?"

"Yes, we did. It's beautiful. All that lovely . . ."

"Where'd we put it?"

"I'll find it." She hurried back toward the TV. "See, it was right up here," she called to us, "on this shelf with my paperwork, because I was reading an article . . ." She brought the magazine to the table and laid it next to the card. "Jay is just a

wonderful, sweet person," she said. "If I'd had children . . ."
She turned away, facing the lake. She was crying. "If only you
hadn't let the cottage go . . ."

Schooltz covered his eyes.

My fist hit the table. But the rest of my body seemed calm,
and my head clear, as I watched the hand open and the fingers
tremble. How could we keep the cottage? We were in love at
the cottage.

"It's ten-thirty," I finally said. "She's been gone at least five
and a half hours, more likely seven or eight. Schooltz, I want
to take your pickup and drive around the lake."

"I'll go with you."

"What if they call and . . ."

"He's right," Mabel said.

The sleet had turned to light flurries and visibility was improved. Also the pickup, sitting high, gave me a better view.
My thinking was: after leaving the cottage she could have decided to take a drive on the road that followed the shoreline
into town, which was the route we always took; it was slower
than the paved two-lane, but prettier, and since she went to the
cottage for that memory, maybe she wanted the shore drive
too. And if she went around midafternoon, the weather was
clear. If she got stuck or ran out of gas or had any other car
trouble, there were two bars along the way she could have
walked to for help. Or she could have simply stopped in one
and be there now, waiting out the storm over a brandy.

I passed the Wolcjacks' cubs, the three white pines where
Ellen watercolored, our place again. I wondered if I should
stop and leave a note in case she went back there, but decided
she would have taken Jenny's key if she planned to return. I

remembered Jenny's system of letting visitors know of our whereabouts when we left the cottage for a few hours: she had made two watercolors—one showing three figures in front of a huge pine, which meant a picnic in a state park, and other an ice cream cone, which meant town; she posted the appropriate picture on the back door. She made the pictures at Ellen's. I could hear Ellen roughly whispering Jenny's name with what was left of her voice after the doctor, operating on her thyroid, cut a vocal cord. If she still had her voice she'd be teaching at the county school instead of going to Arizona every winter, and if Jay was at anyone's house right now on that wretched lake it would be Ellen's.

There were two cars parked in front of the Rustic, neither one a white or cream Fairlane. I described Jay to the bartender. He hadn't seen her but would give her my message if he did. Then I called Schooltz.

"Nothing," he said.

I took a black coffee back to the pickup and burned my tongue drinking too fast. It was eleven o'clock. The farther I drove along that twisting road looking for Iowa plates on the few cars parked beside it, suddenly being passed by whining snowmobiles, their insane engines leaving a ring in my ears, the less confidence I had in my direction. And that busy signal I'd received calling from O'Hare began to nag at me more. I'd thought of it a couple of times in the last few hours, but I didn't know what to do with it. I still didn't. Jay had called someone—or tried to—around two o'clock, but who? I lit a cigarette and fell into a chest-squeezing coughing fit.

In high school, my last year, I was jogging around the track getting my legs in shape for baseball. I was jogging with wiry

Bartholomew, who ran the dashes. I felt good, the air was cool and sweet, the grass starting to green, and after a few laps, without saying anything, we began to push each other, slowly at first, then in earnest, until we were racing—one lap, two, staying even, and just when I felt neither one of us could go on, that we'd "tied," Bartholomew sprinted away as if from a man standing still. When I stopped I dropped to my knees, dry-heaving and belching rancid air, my chest feeling as it did now, stomped on and kicked in a fight I couldn't remember.

Bob's Big Perch Inn was up ahead and I could see a white car parked in front. Yes, yes, yes, I said, hitting the steering wheel, please, baby, please. But it wasn't. And the bartender couldn't be sure he had seen a woman fitting Jay's description.

"Hey, Chuck," he called to a toothpick-chewer playing shuffleboard. "Them two women came in about nine, one of 'em have brown hair or was they both blondes?"

Chuck scattered cornmeal and laughed, feigning innocence. "Shoot, Russell, how comes you always ask *me? I* don't look at other women, the old lady'd run me over." And he laughed again, wagging his toothpick. I wanted to hit him in the face.

"They was blondes, wasn't they?"

"If you say so, Russell."

"Wearing black snowmobile suits with gold trim, if that'll help you," the bartender told me.

I used his phone to call Schooltz.

"Bill, they found the car," he said. "It's up in the Hartwick Pines."

"But not Jay."

"They're looking."

It was midnight when I got back to Schooltz's. He was in

the Olds, the engine running. Mabel handed me two Thermoses—soup and coffee—and a wool blanket. "A ranger found the car," he said. All I could think of right then, sinking into the seat, was how you keep walking in circles.

The Hartwick Pines were thirty miles straight north of us, just above Grayling off Interstate 75. Ten thousand acres of timber, some of it virgin white pine the loggers had somehow missed, and a branch of the Au Sable River winding through. You went to the Pines to hike or snowshoe or cross-country ski, or to take pictures of the replica logger's camp or, if you were lucky, of a Kirtland's warbler. Or to have your picture taken in front of the giant Monarch pine, and to read the plaque beside it which tells you there's enough lumber in that one tree to build a five-room house. But why would you go there, in this weather, if you were Jay? Especially after having driven God knew how many miles already? For the same reason she went to our old cottage, probably; it was another memory. All right. But why was she still there?

"Schooltz, why is she still there?"

"What?" When I didn't answer, he said, angry, "Take a damn snowmobile anywhere. You can't show me the ground I can't drive mine over. They'll find her—God damn it, it's their job."

"I know they will."

"Damn right they will."

I watched the flurries fly at the windshield or looked at the woods on either side of us. I remembered reading somewhere once, maybe on a plaque in the Pines, that there were eighty-five species of trees in Michigan. Or were at one time. I tried to name to myself as many as I could. I got to twenty. I repeated the list and lost two or three, tried again and lost a couple more. At the sign for Grayling, named for a trout long gone from the area, my head filled with a light buzz. Here Jay was wandering somewhere in the middle of ten thousand acres on a night most people would think twice about even taking out the garbage, and I was naming trees in my head like a kid counting cows or barns to pass the time.

"Schooltz," I said, giddy, "I've been counting trees."

"We're almost there."

He turned off the interstate onto the two-lane, M-93. We had only three or four miles to go to the ranger's house. The trees grew closer to the road now, and it was slicker going. Suddenly I thought of something that froze me.

"What if she's not in the park? Schooltz, that car doesn't have to mean *she's* there! What the hell are we doing! It's one o'clock in the morning! You think somebody's going to be walking around in the woods at one o'clock in the morning! Somebody took that car away from her—"

"Calm down."

I shut up, but I was shaking all over. And that busy signal I'd heard at O'Hare came back to me and wanted to mean something. At the ranger's house we parked behind the state police cruiser, its blood-red light revolving, hitting our hood. They were waiting for us.

The next two hours were a play of facts and surmises and questions and answers and explanations and attempts at explanations and bullhorns and whining snowmobiles—mainly whining snowmobiles—all given or asked or offered or called into or driven over trails and roads in scenes that my mind kept sliding away from and coming back to because I had forgot, it occurred to me, to tie my mind down.

The ranger, his wife, a state trooper, Schooltz, and I stood in a circle and some of us held mugs of coffee. The ranger's wife held a small calico cat whose front leg was wrapped in a splint, and the ranger held a pipe that he seemed to want to light but never did. He looked remarkably like my cousin Robert—big shoulders, bull neck, a thick black toothbrush mustache. The state trooper summarized his findings and said there was good reason to believe that the subject was in the park. He never used her name until the very end. Once or twice it occurred to me to request that he say "Jay," but I didn't want to interrupt his recitation. Listening to him calmed me down—to the point, a few times, of even feeling pleasantly drowsy. Also I was grateful that he gave only passing reference to the possibilities of an abduction or a rendezvous with a second party, both of which he seemed to dismiss with his hand. Like the ranger he was big in the shoulders and neck, but twenty years older, perhaps fifty-five, with the slightly gravelly voice of an uncle you liked a great deal.

The car, he said, had been found in the parking lot behind the contact station; normally a ranger would have been posted there during the daylight hours to check vehicles for parking permits, offer assistance, etc., but bad weather the past two days had kept the skiers away—there was very little traffic in the park during the week anyway—and therefore no one had been manning the station. "The car was spotted by a road crew about nine o'clock and reported to the ranger, who called it in to us," the trooper said. He himself had been there since eleven. He found only one set of tracks—excluding the ranger's—near the car. Despite new snowfall, the trooper said he got a pretty good fix on the direction she at least started out in, which was due east to the two-lane, M-93. He managed to pick up the tracks on the other side of it, where they continued east a few yards to the campground, but he lost them there because of some road crew activity in that area and increased snowfall. That direction, he said, if she stayed with it, would eliminate the largest part of the park; almost three-quarters of it. "Of course," he added, "she could have turned back anywhere along the line."

The ranger said, "We checked out the chapel and all the toilets west of 93 anyway—none of those buildings are locked—in case she did turn back. Also all the short trails right around the logging camp."

So they were concentrating the search east of M-93: the Mertz Grade trail, Hartwick Lake, the plowed gravel roads, the lesser roads, the virgin jack pine stand, and the Au Sable trail. They had three snowmobiles out now, and the ranger and the trooper were going back out in a few minutes.

"What can you tell us?" the trooper asked me.

I told him what I'd told Schooltz and Mabel—that when I'd arrived in Des Moines that morning she was gone.

"Wednesday morning," he said.

"That's right. But I tried several times to call her on Tuesday."

He looked at some papers on his clipboard. "She spent Tuesday night in a motel in Holland," he said. "Monday night in Gary, Indiana, and Sunday night in Moline, Illinois. These receipts were in the glove compartment." He paused, sipping coffee. "Not much else in the car—used Kleenex, some apples and cheese, orange peels. The keys were under the front seat."

"That's where we always kept them," I said.

"She's thirty-five years of age."

"Yes. And in good condition. We've skied out here, hiked, I don't know how many times."

"Last seen at two P.M. yesterday in Houghton Lake."

"That's right."

"Any idea why she'd come to the Pines alone?"

I shook my head. "Memories," I said.

There was a long silence. The trooper's eyes were fixed on his clipboard, the ranger's on his unlit pipe, his wife's on her cat, and Schooltz was looking at a snapshot of Jay he'd slipped from his wallet. My legs and head felt loose. Did I tell them Jenny was dead?

Finally the ranger said something about the Mertz Grade.

"I can't believe she'd be on the Mertz," I said, adding, stupidly, "not at night." I tried again, "I mean we never used that trail anymore. In recent years—in the winter—we skied either west, out the Aspen trail, ending up back around the Monarch pine, or out the Au Sable."

The ranger nodded solemnly. "Be difficult knowing where you were, now. Even for an expert."

Schooltz gave the trooper the photograph. In a white gown, white gloves, shoulders bare, orchid corsage on her breast, Jay at seventeen, her eyes filled with a sweet quizzical shine from somebody's flash, is off to the prom. We all stared at her.

Finally the ranger, clearing his throat, said he hoped she stumbled across one of the roads and stayed on it.

His wife said, "You'll find her. I know you will."

After looking at a map, we went outside. The ranger and I would take the Au Sable trail on a snowmobile, while the trooper and Schooltz, in a Jeep, would follow the plowed gravel road which ran almost three-quarters around our trail and ended up back on M-93 about two miles directly north of us.

Our plan was simple. The Au Sable trail forms a large circle slowly collapsing: flat on the bottom, humped twice on top, with fairly parallel sides running north and south. On the map it also resembles a torso with high shoulders (one of the images I forced myself to focus on whenever I felt drowsy). The west side of it, for about a third of its distance, runs within yards of M-93; the other two-thirds, which buckle away from M-93 as much as three or four hundred yards, are still within shouting distance of a dirt road that runs between M-93 and the trail. Almost the entire east side of the trail runs within a hundred yards of the gravel road. In the north, the gravel road was not much good to us, except for a short distance where it cuts back in near the torso's eastern shoulder. That same shoulder is where the Au Sable River enters the torso, and continues on down as if around the heart and over the ribs toward where the left leg would begin. Twice the river passes under footbridges. If she left the trail and wandered due west toward M-93, we were in the best shape. If she wandered due east toward the gravel road, we had a pretty good chance there. South, the gravel road lies perhaps half a mile away at the closest point and a mile at the farthest. We hoped she did not wander south or north. We hoped she was not wandering at all, but waiting somewhere on a trail or walking on a road. Our simple plan was to drive around slowly and stop periodically and call out into the darkness.

The Au Sable trail is over five miles long. We figured to cover it in ninety minutes or less. The ranger, in his snowmobile suit, asked if I was cold. No, I wasn't. It was about five above zero and falling, he said.

The first time we stopped and he cut the motor I couldn't say her name right away. Then when I tried, using my own voice, it sounded as if someone else, a distance away, had called out. My ears were full of that insane engine whine. Also my throat was very dry; I scooped up some snow and ate it. Then I said her name into the bullhorn. "JAAAY." The sound might have been the deep scraping cry of a large bony creature who did not belong in these woods, who did not belong anywhere except in a museum for students to study its skeleton. "ARE YOU THERE, JAAAY?"

We waited half a minute, then started up again. We were following the post markers put down for hikers. Without a light you would not have been able to spot them, and come up close, as we did, and knock the fresh snowcones off and see the deer hooves burned into their tops at an angle. We also saw real deer tracks in our light on the trail, and snow falling through the light, but no human tracks. The farther along we went the thicker the pines grew. When I called out her name against them, the scraping cry seemed to get smothered in the snow collected on their branches. And up in their tops I could hear the wind make a hushed whispering. Be quiet or go away, it seemed to say.

Just before we got to the river we came to a place where the pines grew so close to the trail that their lower branches made a roof over us. The ranger cut the motor and pointed ahead. I saw them—tracks that the new snow hadn't been able to cover completely; soft, regular depressions that rendered us both silent for a moment. Finally I said, "They've got to be hers." He got off the snowmobile for a closer look. "East," he said.

At the river we stopped on the footbridge and I used the bullhorn. It got a good carry here, upstream and down; but after its harsh echoes died away all we heard was the wind above us and the water brushing past boulders under our feet. Less snow was falling in the snowmobile's beam now, and we could see where the moon lay through a skim of clouds.

"We took off our shoes here last summer, and walked upstream to the other bridge," I said. "It was a wonderful walk. We saw a doe leap across the river." I could see her again. I could almost smell her.

He used his radio to report our position, and to ask for news from the other units. One ranger had sighted tracks leaving M-93 north of Hartwick Lake; he pursued these on foot and followed them back to the road, where he lost them. The other units had only snowshoe tracks or signs of snowmobile violations to report. The state trooper said he saw a nice buck, about eight points. I scooped a handful of snow from the bridge's guard rail and rubbed it over my face.

We left the bridge and started up Jay's and my favorite part of the trail, which runs parallel to the river. In the summer walking over the brown pine needles with their slight spongy give and the sun speckled on them, and seeing the airy white rips of the stream only yards away, you felt as though you could walk forever, and why not if it was this good. Then at the second bridge you took off your shoes and lay back with your feet in the water, eating a piece of cheese or an apple and watching the tips of the pines sway easily, or listening to the birds discuss simple matters agreeably, and all of that felt pretty fine too, just being lazy there, getting drowsy in the sun; and after a while you pulled your feet up out of the stream and worked your shoulders into a good position on the warm pine planks and fell asleep; and if someone was with you she was doing the same thing.

In the winter the trail was lovely in other ways—the sun shone brightly off the snow collected on the pine boughs, and the river, when you were beside it, was a bright black swiftly moving thing among the snow-covered boulders and fallen tree trunks, and you worked your skis and poles in a steady rhythm and felt used in the best way you could think of—used and lucky and happy in your juices. But now the trail looked like any other place you'd see in the woods at night on a whining snowmobile—an alley with dark tree-shapes on either side; or if you closed your eyes and pictured the map, the left side of the torso.

"JAAAY!" I called. And the scraping cry of the bony creature echoed and died, echoed and died.

When we came to the second bridge and found nothing to indicate she'd been there, I started to shiver and could not stop. The ranger took the bullhorn and said, "MRS. RAU, DO YOU HEAR ME? ONE, TWO, THREE, FOUR. DO YOU HEAR ME, MRS. RAU?"

I looked upstream and tried to see where the doe had leaped across last summer, but the river beyond the bridge was just a black ribbon laid down between dark cloud-like masses. I began to mumble. If I said words I don't remember them, but I know I made sounds with my mouth because the ranger kept saying, "What? What's that?" And I remember him turning around and taking off his helmet. Finally I stopped. His radio crackled and buzzed and he talked to it, soothing it. Or maybe he was talking to me. The next thing I remember is crossing the bridge, leaving the place where ever since the first bridge I had expected to find her.

Now we were riding down into the valley of the torso's neck. It was part cedar swamp and then scrub pine and the trail was very narrow. Twice we passed under low branches that formed roofs over our heads, but in neither place did we see any signs of tracks. That made no sense to me. I said so the first time, but the ranger said she could have left the trail at any point after passing under those pines where we'd spotted the tracks. Still I did not think so, and the farther we went the more nervous I got, while he seemed to become more matter-of-fact, or perhaps just tired. It was almost three o'clock. Each time we stopped I had to wash my face with snow.

We stopped again and just before I used the bullhorn I saw fresh deer tracks at the edge of our beam; the back of my neck felt suddenly warm, and in a place in my head it was summer and the doe was leaping across the river. When she was midstream I called, "I WANT TO GO BACK TO THE SECOND BRIDGE! I WANT TO GO BACK TO THE SECOND BRIDGE!" The ranger turned and asked if we shouldn't finish the trail first, and with the bullhorn still at my month I said, "NO. THERE'S A PLACE I HAVE TO LOOK!"

Whether he thought I was on the edge of losing control and the only way to calm me down was to return, or whether he thought I had a solid hunch we ought to check out, he drove us back. At the bridge I got off the snowmobile and directed him to position it so that I could have some light along the river's east bank. He followed me as far as he could into the thick brush, maybe fifteen yards. That's all the help I needed, because twenty or thirty yards beyond that, under the roots of a cedar tree that had been pushed half over, I found her. Lying curled on her side with an urn of ashes in her arms. Breathing.

5

Dawn in late winter up north the sky is often a walleye gray, and a coon may be just outside the door to show you the fish head he plucked from your Grape Nuts box. He's met you there at the garbage can several mornings now and seems to have forgotten his role as thief, though he does turn finally and give you his back, embarrassed perhaps to take the last bite in front of your face. Then he jumps to the ground and scurries off. It has become almost civilized, this congress with the coon; all that's lacking is speech. Walking along the lake, waking up slowly, you wonder what would be a good thing to say to him next time.

But there was no next time. Maybe the solar eclipse did something to his rhythms. Or maybe he just found better pickings. Or maybe a big-gamer shot him.

That February morning when the eclipse occurred I was replacing the glass I'd busted in the door of our former cottage. The sun was between the two Norway pines a little to my right, around eleven o'clock in the sky, and I was tacking down the new molding. Although I knew it was foolish, I wanted to look at the eclipse. The snow in the yard grew gradually grayer, a color darker than the gray squirrel that darted past the door, returned, then sat on his haunches regarding me, working his paws to no purpose. Behind him, the woods across the road seemed one-dimensional, fake, like a painted backdrop for an eerie play. Everything seemed fake, even the squirrel. I wondered if he was a descendant of General Buck, a squirrel Jay used to feed.

Thinking about Jay and the squirrel I looked up at the sun, a piercing hump of white that held me close enough to kiss it. When I turned away I felt dizzy. I dropped my hammer and in the kitchen sat at the table, rubbing my eyes. Bright white bubbles were bursting in my brain. They were filled with sand, it felt like, and the sand was hot and scratching the backs of my eyeballs. I put my head down, the way we used to at school, after our milk.

Jay and General Buck came forward and bowed to each other. She fed him the walnuts and almonds we bought to mix in our cereal. He got fat as a badger. Then the Darks appeared in the cottage next door, to hammer and saw and prune on weekends. Mr. Dark called his son Dummy. I forgot what his Christian name was, but I did remember he was in pharmacy school. Mrs. Dark gave off a rooster call when something tickled her. They had a poodle named George and Mrs. Dark said, "He's really the boy's dog, but he prefers mother's company." She said that often and every time she said it she gave off the rooster call.

One day Mr. Dark yelled, "Spread that sand *even*, Dummy!" They were filling in a marshy area where mosquitoes bred. The next morning Jay found General Buck at the base of a silver maple, his shoulder ripped raw by a slug. My eyes felt scratched for a week.

Our second year in the Upper Peninsula when we lived in Brown's storybook house, there was a young man named Chester who lived three doors away. In nice weather he sat on his porch wearing a black beret and played chess against himself. In the yard at the side of his house stood two elm stumps, each one large enough for a man and woman to get up on and dance, which is what Jay and I did one night the autumn Jenny was growing in her belly—carefully, a slow two-step—before we knew Chester's story.

Brown told it to us. He was soaking Spooker's swollen paw in milk, and maybe the milk made him think of the clouds Chester's eyes became after he dashed out from behind one of the elms at age four and his father, testing a new lure for its weight and carry, hooked him. "Infection," Brown said, "took the other eye."

As I write, I am sitting on a rock on Dunvegan Head on the west coast of Skye, looking across the Strait of Little Minch toward islands I do not see—North Uist, South Uist, Barra, Saint Kilda. And thinking of the castle I passed on my way up here, of the old mansion we've found to stay in, and of Louis the Eleventh of France washing the feet of his beloved greyhounds in warm wine.

Jay gave me that piece of history three nights ago; Louis' favorite greyhound, she said, wore robes and slept in a bed.

The mansion also has dogs, the Colonel's black and white collies that follow him everywhere, even to his large four-poster, where the old one, Mollie, trembles against him whenever a storm is gathering at the top of the Sound of Raasay. "She's as deaf as I am," he says, "but she can tell when we're due." Mollie occupies the second pillow, while her sons, Brittle and Glenn, warm his feet.

The Colonel is eighty-nine, his wife perhaps fifteen years

younger. We found them after taking a wrong turn in the Trot-ternish, and for two weeks now we have slept in their guest room which overlooks the dovecote and, farther out, the stand of pines where the Colonel's buzzards nest. Jay says she could live in the Colonel's house forever. I believe her. When we stood in the entrance that first day, regarded by the bearcat and Bengal tiger frozen in their full snarls, by the almost life-size oils of Scottish chiefs and their women hung among the mounted horns of stags and ibex and mountain sheep and the stuffed carcasses of hawks and eagles and owls in postures of striking, and not least regarded by the heavy dark stilled faces of three large walnut and ebony clocks, which stand taller than I do and resemble caskets, and a fourth clock, a squat, more jovial job, resting beside a huge wire cage from which the crazy chorus of a dozen parakeets cried out—when we stood, as I say, confronted by this menagerie, Jay clutched at my arm and whispered, "I think I'm entering a story," and her eyes, excited, were ready for it.

The big bell beside the jovial clock bore a sign which said, "Ring." We rang it. The old woman who appeared, leaning hard on her cane, might have fallen out of one of the oils. She was large in voice and bosom and spoke the kind of English you hear in old movies telling of the Empire's thrust over mountain, desert, and plain to civilize whatever it finds. She would civilize us, too, I felt, if we had character and paid enough attention.

"You've come for a room, have you? Well, I think we can manage. Unfortunately you've missed dinner, but we're gathering for tea in the drawing room around ten."

After a word about the room, she pointed her cane at the

long staircase and left us. Now, up here in the sea air on Dunvegan Head, among the grazing sheep and the lambs butting under their mothers' bellies for milk, I remember also, on the staircase as we ascended, how Jay's neck seemed suddenly very white, the long smooth curve of it under her newly cropped and banged and blackened hair taking me back to Marquette, to our final summer there when she had her hair cut to look as it does now, as it has since April when we finally found where to put Jenny's ashes. Is the connection I'm moving toward too subtle? Let me try again: we released her, gave her up to the water and rocks and those sudden cold springs that once made her jump, squealing, in delight, and then we looked in the mirror of the old vanity opposite the high wide bed that the Colonel's wife said we would be happy in, and saw ourselves coming closer, my hair longer than hers now, and my hands and then my lips on her neck as if fourteen years and everything else hadn't happened. Except that we were actors, mimes, performing for no one but ourselves, cool, polished, raw, athletic, and wordless. But let me finish this: the first time Jay came home in her glossy black helmet, Jenny had recently been baptized; the second time, three months ago, was after the burial ceremony in the river. Isn't she aware of that sad ironic symmetry? Or am I expecting something from her—and from myself—that isn't there?

She was in the hospital for two weeks. She was sleeping and her face looked blue when the doctor finally let me go in. Later, half awake, she said, "I was the Answer Girl . . . on the radio . . . one of those phone-in programs . . . someone kept calling in . . ." Then she closed her eyes, which were large and sickly bright and seemed separate from the rest of her, and the nurse indicated I should leave. I thought they were lying to me, that she was dying. I left Schooltz and Mabel at the hospital, walked around Grayling for a while, and when I came back her Filipino doctor was laughing about something with a nurse. He had a gold tooth like Poppy's. I watched Schooltz rub his stubs until I couldn't sit in the lounge any longer, and went up and stood in the hall outside her room.

Through the door behind me, in another room, Fred Fry sat with his wife. Every day during Jay's first week in the hospital, Fred Fry, a carpenter, sat with his wife from early morning until late at night. I never heard her say anything, but a couple of times I heard him say, "Naw, now, don't you worry. The only job I got's this awful bugger, and they can wait." His wife seemed forgotten by a puppeteer who simply tied his end of the strings somewhere above her bed, she had that many tubes running into her. The day they took down the strings and told Fred they were sorry, I made a short meaningless list of carpenters—Fred, Joseph, my old man, Bruno Hauptmann, Halvard Solness, and the one Jay sat in judgment of last summer, the one her fellow juror felt should be given the benefit of doubt. I can think of a lot more now, but there's still no point to it.

"We used to have the secret, didn't we, Billy?" She was watching the snow fly against the window. I don't know how long I stayed that time—perhaps an hour—and I don't remember anything else she said. Maybe she didn't say anything else. We watched the snow, and silently I agreed: we did, yes, have the secret once.

The secret on Skye, a crofter hinted to us, may be held by the Old Man of Storr, who stands with his companions, or family, leaning eerily toward the Sound of Raasay on the east side of the island, in the Trotternish, where Jay and I wandered those first days after we arrived. We did not know, then, that he had a name, though we should have known because he at least, the tallest of the dark torso-like figures frozen in a lonely attitude facing the sea, cried out for one; and Jay supplied it, "Mr. Monk." Later, dwarfed among them with our wine and cheese, winded from the pace we'd set climbing up, we decided they were all monks.

"And they ruled Skye for hundreds of years," Jay said. "Just them and the sheep. And back there behind the mountain, in a huge stone warehouse, are all the wool sweaters and socks they knitted, waiting for the tourists."

"But the tourists didn't come right away."

"No, they didn't. They weren't born yet," she said.

"Who did come, then?"

"The Scots! With their bagpipes. That's when bagpipes, incidentally, entered history. And the sound of *those,* of course— well, you can see what it did to the poor monks."

"Froze them."

"Do you mean froze as in *stunned?*"

"Yes."

"Yes, that's correct," she said.

"Where does Bonnie Prince Charlie fit into this story?"

"Well, contrary to the official view, he came over not to hide from the English but to thaw out these monks. He had a magic potion."

"And Flora Macdonald's role?"

"Figure it out." She gave me a sly look.

"Explain it to me. You're the historian."

"And *you're* the poet, for criminey's sake!"

"Criminey's sake. Nobody talks like that anymore."

We sat down among the stone figures, facing the sea with them, and opened the wine. The sun was straight up and warm and we felt suddenly relaxed, more at ease with each other than we'd felt in weeks. Five days ago we were in London, before that New York, seeing a musical or two, a baseball game, the big soccer match between England and Scotland for the British Isles championship, walking dozens of blocks to a bar we thought we remembered, a minor tourist attraction on the map, maybe finding them, taking pictures of the Cloisters, Yankee Stadium, Big Ben, saying, without much humor, that we were slow hicks from the Midwest, TV quiz show winners spending their dream vacation prize in the big city, art-farts taking slides of culture for the local library back home, and finally, tiring of the games, just our weary and walked-out selves, whoever we were; but calling no one we knew, a subject we never even brought up, for whatever this trip meant it included, by tacit agreement, just the two of us. Even now, on Skye, I'm still not sure what our purpose is. Maybe we're simply running away, killing time—or trying to. Or maybe, in a queer way, we *are* those game show winners we mimicked, spending not the latest magic detergent loot but Jay's retirement money.

*

The light, coming from behind, met my glasses at such an angle that I could see Jay and one of my own pupils in the same image. She was sitting up in the hospital bed, holding the yellow rose I brought, her skin not blue anymore and her eyes cleared of that bright sickly shine. The pupil I saw in the corner of my lense was huge and bulbous, a consumptive's. I moved away from the window, losing the double image, and looked at only her.

"Have you been nice to the doctor?" she said.

"We talked some baseball. He's a Tigers fan and mad they got rid of Willie Horton."

"Do you know what I was thinking about before you came? Our first year in Marquette when we got hooked on that bingo game, at the supermarket."

"They had us by the choppers."

"Two and three times a day we went to the store. Some days more. I can't even remember what the prize was."

"It didn't matter."

"It didn't, did it?"

"We were playing against that endless winter."

"They should have said spring was the prize—we'd have gone ten times a day! And we always had just one more square to cover. Remember how we'd be sitting at home and ten minutes before the store closed get a craving for something? I knew what I always wanted—a Sara Lee cheese cake!" She laughed.

"I do remember."

"But we never got our square covered. We just weren't lucky." She pressed that hot-house rose to her cheek, and I thought of how I used to hold a dandelion under her chin to see if she liked butter. But where can you find a dandelion in January! You go to the flower shop and buy what they have from the big vase in the cooler, like everyone else, and then you go to the hospital and remember things from a long time ago—supermarket games and dandelions.

"What should we do with the ashes, Billy?"

"We'll take care of them."

"I was thinking about them before you came. Are they OK?"

"They're at your dad's. In my room."

"I didn't know what to do with them after you left. And then I remembered . . ."

I sat on the bed, by her feet.

". . . walking up the Au Sable last summer, the three of us . . ."

She stopped then and began pulling the petals off the rose, slowly, absently, gazing toward the window, beyond which a squirrel sat on a black limb, his tail muffling his back from the wind. Looking at her eyes I thought of the picture that Schooltz gave to the trooper: in a white gown, white gloves, shoulders bare, orchid corsage on her breast, Jay at seventeen was off to the prom, but before she left Schooltz caught her with a flash, filling her eyes with a sweet quizzical shine that would find one home on top of Aunt Victoria's piano in Pontiac and another in her father's back pocket. Now that shine was appearing here, in a hospital room in a town named for a trout that had gone, above hot-house rose petals adrift on the sheet between our hands like canoes.

I told Schooltz about Jenny as we followed the ambulance from the Hartwick Pines to Grayling. He brought the car to a stop beside the road, opened his door, but did not move. We sat there and watched the red taillights of the ambulance disappear. Snow fell through the funnel of our beams and blew inside the car and settled on the instrument panel. I asked him to let me tell the others. He said nothing, just rubbed his stubs against the steering wheel. Finally he wiped his face on his sleeve, closed the door, and pulled back on the road.

A week later in the hospital lounge I told Mabel. I can't

explain why I waited a week. Maybe because I knew how her face would hang and tremble, and the way she would carry on, shaking her head back and forth, and I put it off as long as I could. Maybe because she panicked when Missy bit the poodle last summer. Nor do I know why I chose the moment Schooltz went outside to walk with the widower Fry.

"Today is my birthday," Mabel finally said, covering her mouth, still shaking her head.

I told her I was sorry; I hadn't remembered.

Other acts of mine that day puzzle me as well. Walking around Grayling I bought twenty-five rounds—a box—of Super-X twenty-gauge high-velocity shotgun shells. Also a red corduroy hunting cap and a bowie knife in a sheath. That night after Schooltz and Mabel went to bed, I got his Remington from the hall closet and back in my room slipped it out of the case. It had been twenty-six years since I'd fired a gun—or even held one. It occurs to me now that a man with a similar record and obsessed by symmetry or ritual, or maybe just superstitious, might have bought twenty-six shells, and then gone outside on a fine day and fired his twenty-six Super-X twenty-gauge high-velocity shotgun shells into the blue sky of his private anniversary. But what I had in mind then I can't say, unless it was simply to keep together as a group the shells, cap, knife, sheath, and my reflection looking at the five of us in the shop's window display.

Schooltz kept his gun cleaned and oiled, though I knew he hadn't used it for years. Largely because of Jay's feelings about hunting. The stock was dark walnut with a good grain finish that reminded me of the arms on my rocking chair that had gone up in flames, tiger stripes, highly polished. I could see my fingerprints on the stock. Fixing the gun under my chin I looked down the barrel, drawing a bead on this and that around the room, my boots on the floor, my red cap on the bureau, an award that Schooltz got from his Lions Club, a picture of Schooltz and Mabel on his snowmobile, a picture of Jay in her high school graduation gown, my own image in the mirror, hunched over, one eye squeezed shut, and my elbows stuck out as if I'd just been rammed in the shoulder by the blue thing I held and any second would fall back. I dropped the gun on the bed. Then, quickly, I wiped my prints off the stock with the sheet, put the gun in its case, and returned it to the hall closet. I could hear Schooltz consoling Mabel, saying, "I know . . . I know . . ."

What did he know? That Jenny's death was sad? That Jay and I were sad, having lost the secret? That Fred Fry, carpenter, was sad, having only an awful bugger of a job to occupy his life now? That sad people don't look real? That somebody pulled the rug out? The plug out? It's like you're moving along, doing what you do, thinking this is where I am, who I am, it's summer, that's a cardinal in the sycamore, singing *UR-be, UR-be*— and presto!—it's winter, a coon is chewing a soup bone, and why is the ice on the lake so black?

"Who do you want to be?" I asked Jay.

We had come out of the grove of white birch that lay a mile as the crow flies from Schooltz's place, to the old softball field. Most of the snow that collected there over the winter was gone—not much stuck to the field anyway, because of the way the winds worked in the lee of the birch grove—so we had enough bare ground to play on. At the Houghton Lake Sports Shop I had picked up a Hillerich & Bradsby glove and ball, both made in Taiwan, and a Louisville Slugger bat made in Kentucky. For three nights running I oiled the glove with neat's-foot and smacked the ball in its pocket, over and over, then left the two of them tied up snug with heavy cord while Jay and I slept. Now she was stronger, it was a nice sunny March day, and so here we were, all set for a little game of pepper.

"Who do I want to be?" she said.

"Yeah. Rizzuto, Appling, George Kell—you can be anybody. Infielders are good for pepper, but you can be whoever you want."

"Babe Ruth, I guess."

"OK. Let's play some catch first. Warm up your wing. Here, Babe, take the glove."

"Who are you?"

"Johnny Lipon. My hero when I was eleven. Slick afield but C+ at the plate. Throw easy, that's it."

"Do I have to call you Johnny Lipon?"

"Of course. We're not good enough yet to be ourselves. Look, see how I push off my right foot when I throw, and step forward with my left? If you stand flat-footed your arm does all the work."

"Like this?"

"Better. But let your wrist go loose, and follow through. You're throwing like a girl."

"Oh dear."

"Hey, look. You want to be a ballplayer?"

"But it slipped out of my hand."

"Shake off the bad throws. They're going to happen. But don't say 'Oh dear,' OK?"

"What should I say when I goof up?"

"'Myfault'— fast like that, one word. Then bear down and get the next one right. That sting?"

"A little."

"Catch it in the webbing."

"I'm trying."

"Step *out,* step *out* with your left.'"

"I keep forgetting, Billy."

"Johnny Lipon, remember?"

"Johnny Lipon."

"Stop crying . . . and watch. I'm going to exaggerate my motion. You ready? I said are you ready?"

"Yes."

"OK. Here it comes. I'm pushing off my right foot—stepping out with the left—and following *through.* See that?"

"I dropped the ball again."

"I know you dropped the ball. But did you see?"

"I don't think I can do it right."

"Of course you can. Use your whole body. Don't worry about the ball going straight. Get your motion smooth and the ball'll know what to do. OK, I'll be Birdie Tebbetts—he was a catcher—and you be Dizzy Trout."

"Dizzy . . . ?"

"Trout. A pitcher. Wore glasses and didn't cry, for Chrissakes. Now pick up the ball and fire it to me."

I knew I was being rotten but I couldn't stop myself. First there was that Bible I found in our bedroom, placed on the bureau beside my red hunting cap and bowie knife. Inside Mabel had written, "To Our Children With All Our Love, Dad and Mother." I put it on the closet shelf next to the box of shotgun shells and covered them both with a blanket. Then came the leaflets from their church—some left in our bedroom, some placed on the coffee and reading tables in the main room—"Marriage and Sickness," "Jesus—Prophet and Profit," "A Happiness Checklist." The inscribed Bible and the leaflets weren't Jay's fault, but there they were, in my head.

Finally we gave up playing catch and went to the Rustic for brandies. I said to Jay, "I wish they'd drop the religious crap."

"It's Mabel. She's just trying to help us."

"Help us, how?"

"I don't know."

"Tell her to quit—or we're leaving."

"Let's do leave, Billy."

"I promised Schooltz we'd stay till you're strong."

"I *am* strong."

"What about the pepper game we didn't even get to play?"

"You're not being fair."

"We've got some things to do yet, anyway."

Back at Schooltz's we were just inside the door when Mabel, in the living room, called, "Jay! Bill! Come look, hurry!"

They were watching the Junior Miss Pageant on TV, and Oklahoma's blonde hope was performing her talent: the Lord's Prayer in Cherokee sign language. When she finished Mabel, shaking her head, her eyes misty, said, "Wasn't that *won*derful!"

*

In the morning, a Saturday, I got up early and drove to Flint, home of the Buick, C. S. Mott, Freddy Zielinski, and Thread Lake where the spiky bullheads oozed. I used to spend a lot of time around Thread Lake, even went swimming in it once when the public pool beside it was closed and came home with muck in my ears and the fear I'd caught polio, like Butch Spa-luka, who hobbled out to right field with an aluminum nail in his good knee to keep that leg short as the bad one. In the ballpark at Thread Lake, batting left-handed, I'd laid down a perfect drag bunt, racing the ball to first with surprise and pride, wondering if any major league scouts were in the stands. I was eleven then, a shortstop. The next year I was a pitcher, like Freddy. He taught me how to throw a round-house curve, passing it on from his old man, a bone-thin dignified gent who made his living as a schoolhouse janitor and who asked Freddy, over and over, not to say "ain't." When Freddy's wife left him and the old man brought him back home, he was less critical of Freddy's English. They'd sit on the porch drinking Goebel's beer and listen to the Tigers. But before that, for seven sum-mers Freddy and I were a pair of pitching fools, from Midget League to American Legion. Never mind that we lit each oth-er's farts, or copped stuff from Max Bender's store, or that Freddy was the first boy on my block to carry a rubber in his wallet and I envied him; when we were fifteen we threw no-hitters, back to back, in a double-header against the fierce black Braves from the North End, and got our smiling choppers in the *Journal*, heroes.

Those are some of the things I thought about while driving Schooltz's Oldsmobile to Flint to tell my family about Jenny.

They didn't know I was coming, nor that I was even in Mich-igan. If I'd called ahead, my mother would have organized a gathering at her place. I just wanted to get her and Andy and Francie and Helen together (and Helen's Frank if he wasn't working, which he almost always was) and tell them. And then, I didn't know what. Have a drink? Go see Freddy? Fly down to Florida and watch the Tigers work out, see an exhibition game or two? I'd never done that. I shouldn't have borrowed Schooltz's car—I couldn't just leave it in Flint while I flew off somewhere. Well, I could return it, then go to Florida. Why did I have to figure out what I was going to do after I told them? I didn't even know if Freddy still lived in Flint, or was even alive. I was a junior in college the last time I saw him— twenty years ago. "Hey, Freddy, how you doing? Long time no see. How's the old arm?" What would we talk about? Why I stopped coming to see him? "Yeah, Fred, I come back to Flint now and again, but it's always a quick shot in, quick shot out. See my mother and brother and sister, and all their kids, you know, and by then I have to leave. Haul my butt up north to stretch out on the skis, hike around, swim, maybe fish a little— just get away, you know? Sit on my ass too long I get pimples on it. That's why I haven't been around to drink a beer, Fred."

I pulled into Andy's driveway and parked behind his pickup. Alec, his son, was shooting baskets in his jacket, cap, and gloves. When he saw me he stood holding the ball until I got out of the car.

"Uncle Bill!"

"Hello, Alec. How's your eye?"

"Oh, pretty good." He passed the ball to me. I bounced it a few times, then went up for a jumper. I missed everything.

"We didn't know you were in Flint, Uncle Bill."

"Came for some roundball. Here, let me have another shot." I missed, hitting the rim, and went in for the rebound. Missed the layup too. "Man, I am *stiff*."

"Where's Aunt Jay and Jenny?"

"Let me see your jumper, Alec, my boy."

"Aw, it's not too good with all these clothes on."

"Try it anyway."

He put the ball up. *Swish.*

"Not bad."

"Yeah, but I feel pretty clumsy. Are they over at Grandma's?"

"Nope. OK, one on one. You drive."

He dribbled toward me, threw an eye-fake left, then went around the arm I flapped at him like a chicken wing, and banked the ball in.

"Nice work."

"Thanks, Uncle Bill."

I grabbed him suddenly by the shoulders and glared. "Why're you so damn polite, kid!"

"Huh?"

"Get tough, buddy boy, or get out!"

"Hey, Uncle Bill, what's the joke?"

Forcing a laugh, I patted him on the cap. My hands were shaking. "Saw some dumbo do that on TV," I lied. "You watch TV?"

"Not too much."

I dribbled the ball in place, hard, until I relaxed a little. Then I dribbled back to the pickup—about twenty feet from the basket. "Three seconds left, Alec. Bill Rau, All-Parochial, goes for it!"

I missed.

"Your mom and dad home?"

"They went shopping. To buy Val a new coat for Easter. I didn't want to go—she takes too long to make up her mind."

"How is your sister?"

"Same."

"Suppose Grandma's home?"

"We can go see."

Alec and I walked up the street to my mother's house. She didn't answer our knock, but her car was in the garage.

"Oh, now I remember," Alec said. "She was going shopping with Aunt Helen and the girls." He rolled his eyes. "I guess they're *all* buying Easter outfits today."

We went back to Andy's. The sky was graying up, getting ready to dump. Alec bounced the ball.

"Want to play some more, Uncle Bill?"

"Don't think so. I've got an errand to run. Tell your mom and dad I'll be back."

I got on Dort Highway, drove past the offerings of potables, chewables, wearables, hearables, visuals, bowlables, gasables, wrenchables, and breakables that are available along its flanks, then turned off for Burton Township—or what used to be called Burton Township—and my old neighborhood.

Everything seemed shrunk, in shabby miniature, except maybe the chuckholes in the streets. Did it look this poor the last time? This *defeated*? I couldn't remember, exactly. But surely there must have been signs, because what I did then—ten years ago? fifteen?—was drive straight through, afraid to stop, I think, and see close up that the landscape of my boyhood might not be there. Now, even in the car, I could see that it wouldn't be. Wasn't. The houses all looked as though they'd been shouted at, humiliated, and then squeezed and whacked deeper into the ground by a giant fist. Their front yards, which once seemed plenty big enough, were small and muddy and almost all of them taken over by rusting-out trailers and trucks and broken-down cars resting on cement blocks; and the empty lot where Freddy had taught me how to twist off the curveball was nothing, a patch of brown winter weeds maybe long enough to park two Oldsmobiles on, bumper to bumper. The house I grew up in seemed shrunk and squeezed as the others. A Cyclone fence had been put around it, in case, I supposed, the giant fist returned. Inside the fence a large black split-eared dog paced back and forth, and the three towering elms that used to shade our driveway were gone.

I pulled up in front of Freddy's old house and looked at the porch where he and his father listened to the Tigers. The porch ran the width of the house and, like it, used to be covered with a clean white wood siding that Mr. Zielinski scraped and repainted every three years. Now all that white was covered with sheeting the color of avocado. I went up and knocked, and after two or three minutes stood looking through the aluminum storm door at Mr. Zielinski, in a wheel chair like Freddy's. He must have broken his hip or something, I thought. But except for the wheelchair he looked as he did twenty years ago—the skull-shaped face and bald dome, a few white hairs, neatly combed, above the jug ears, a mouthful of cheap pinkish false teeth that were too big for him, and those bone-thin arms that had pulled in so many fish and moved with such authority over his head and across his chest when demonstrating a "major league" windup. They hung, now, limply beside the wheels. We sat and stood on either side of the door for maybe a minute, taking each other in, both of us smiling awkwardly and shaking our heads. Then he said, "Well, hot damn, if it ain't Bill Rau!" and I knew it was Freddy.

Here on Dunvegan Head I prefer to think of another meeting, our first, on a bright early summer day like this one. He was out in his yard with a jar catching bees, and I stood by our grapevines watching, hoping he'd notice and invite me over. We'd just moved to Flint from up north and I didn't have any playmates yet. Creeping among the dandelions, he gradually worked his way closer to our grapevines. He was shirtless and his big ears stuck out from under his baseball cap. I took off my shirt too and wished I had a cap like his, with that unusual letter on it. Finally we were looking at each other, and talking. He came up next to the vines and showed me the bees, explaining you had to take a nail and drive holes in the jar's lid or the bees'd keel over. He was going to keep them awhile—feed them sugar water—and then let them go. They weren't good for anything, he said, except to put your ear up next to the lid and listen to them buzz. Unless you caught a queen, then you could start a hive. But he wasn't interested in that; his dad knew a man who got stung all over by a swarm and went crazy. Then Freddy handed the jar across the vines so I could put my ear next to the lid. That was the beginning of our friendship, listening to those furious bees and hearing, as Freddy predicted, "the hundred ocean roars" he said they sounded like.

But sitting in the avocado-colored house his mother had left him—she died the previous fall, two years after his father—we never got around to remembering the bees, or the night crawlers we pulled from their holes with our hands that we'd rubbed in ashes, or the pails of bluegills we plucked from the Mill Pond in Atlas, or sledding down Lyle's Hill, or, capped and gloved like Alec, shooting baskets against his garage long after dark, careful not to let our jumpers get away and put out the one vulnerable bulb that craned over naked from the gable, or the back-to-back no-hitters, or sneaking bottles of his old man's

Goebels the Saturday nights I stayed at his house, hearing him describe how when he was younger and scared by a storm he'd get into bed with Phyllis, his older half sister, taking a flashlight with him and crawling under the covers to see what she had. What we—he—talked about was the book he fetched from a table and gripped in his lap, the stories in it about people who said they had died and come back to life.

"I believe every one of them," he said, "and I'll tell you why. Because *I* died eighteen months ago—right here in this room— and what do you see now? Cleo witnessed it!"

I nodded, as if I saw and understood and believed too; but in a corner of my head I was thinking of him as he stood on the other side of our grapevines, saying, "Cleo's my mother. I call her Cleo the Cow because her eyes are bulgy and brown. She's my dad's second wife and I'm their only kid. But he's got two other kids—girls—older than me. The one that lives here—you'll see her—she's got fifty boyfriends." The same boy who, explaining the Old English D on his cap, said, "That's a Detroit D—for Detroit Tigers. I'm going to play for them."

He went on with his story. "They said I'd had a heart attack—from the shock of getting all my teeth yanked at once. That may be so. But I'll tell you, like I told them, that I was dead. Gone. Bill, I wasn't even *here* for most of it. I was over in Goodrich, where my dad died fishing. He was waiting for me. I left my body slumped down in this chair and drifted up to the ceiling in another body—a *good* body—drifted right across there," he pointed above my head, "then out the door and on over to Goodrich. When I saw my dad he said, 'Tell Cleo I'm waiting for her.' Those were his exact words, Bill," and Freddy repeated them, slowly, solemnly, as if their full meaning would not come through to me—or to him—on only one profane hearing. Then he shook his head and looked toward the picture of his mother.

Cleo Zielinski was a small bird-like woman whose pretty brown eyes *were* bulgy. In the portrait of her that Freddy kept on the TV set, next to a portrait of his father, she was holding in her lap a small powder blue poodle (whose eyes were miniatures of hers, confusing the bird-like image I remembered) and looking at us as if we had just asked her a question she ought to be able to answer but, for the life of her, couldn't. Her brow was furrowed with fuzzy lines, shadows of deeper, sharper worry that the airbrush couldn't remove, and frustration lightly pocked her chin and tightened her lips. Her hair, however, was the party color of the poodle's and almost as curly, her cheeks were brightly rouged, and around her neck she wore the gold cross that Freddy bought her for the sitting. He knew she would soon be with her husband twenty miles away in Goodrich and he wanted a good picture to remember her by. He said, proudly, "That's just how she looked when she fixed herself up." Soon after she died he had Skipper, the poodle, put to sleep, in the firm belief the dog would join its mistress.

When Freddy and I said good-bye, he tried to give me the book in his lap. I told him I was pretty sure I had a copy at home. It was a sloppy lie, I mean I told it sloppy, and he looked puzzled and hurt. Shaking hands I could feel more bones in his grip than living flesh. As I drove away I knew I would never see him again.

In my mother's house there were no portraits on her television set. A thing made of clear yellow glass and filled with liquid was displayed there—a thing resembling a large fat thumbless palm whose four fingers pointed skyward. When plugged in, the thing warmed and the liquid sent a stream of bubbles up and down each finger. My mother bought it last summer, she told me, shortly after my birthday party; she said it was nice company sometimes and also complemented her color set. She turned it on for me and the fingers bubbled and bubbled that afternoon when I returned from Freddy's house to tell her about Jenny.

They bubbled while the rain fell and the room darkened and I struggled for a way to begin. She had asked where Jay and Jenny were, of course, and I said, "At Houghton Lake." Why hadn't I brought them with me? "I decided to come to Flint at the last minute, alone," I said. Had I eaten? "Yes." I asked how her shopping trip went. She said she was tired, she had a headache; nothing fit, or it was too expensive, or Helen's girls were more interested in jeans and sweatshirts than nice dresses. Was anything wrong? What were we doing in Michigan this time of year? "We decided to sell the cottage." Was I sure I didn't want a sandwich or something? She had a nice roast she could thaw out. "Yes, I'm sure." So, we were getting rid of the cottage, well it was probably a headache anyway. All that work Dad put into it.

"I'll have a drink with you, though," I said, and fixed two bourbons from the bottle I brought. She turned on the television—there was a Bette Davis movie at four o'clock she wanted to see. How were Schooltz and Mabel? Was Mabel still fat? "They're fine," I said. She herself had lost weight, could I tell? Now none of her clothes fit. Well, it wasn't much fun cooking for one person. My God, was *that* Bette Davis! She really looked *rough*. At a commercial she'd take that roast out of the freezer. "Please don't bother, Mother, I can't stay."

So I was driving back to Houghton Lake tonight? In this weather? Well, I could suit myself. She was just going to watch TV, maybe heat up some leftovers. She was used to being alone. By the way, our Christmas presents were in the hall closet. I could take them with me when I went. She hoped Jenny liked what she got her. She was sick during Christmas and couldn't get out to mail them. Couldn't do anything this year. Now all she did lately was lock the doors and turn off the lights and watch TV. And eat leftovers. She'd made a nice dinner for Andy and Francie last Sunday and they left half of it. Diets! Everybody's on a diet but they can drink champagne! Ten dollars for a bottle of champagne. Andy bought her one for New Year's . . . it sat in the refrigerator for weeks! One night she got blue and drank the son of a bitch. It made her sicker than a dog you'd see vomiting on the street.

*

The thing about the Old Man of Storr, whether he knows the secret or not, is the sense of *waiting* that seems to hover in the air around him. And around the others too, of course, and around us when we sit among them. But there is nothing unpleasant or nervous about the waiting, not even at dusk when the browns and greens in the mountains deepen and join and the shadows lengthen; when the clusters of sheep, dark bubbly shapes, slowly rise and slowly, slowly dip toward the black pools of the inland lochs. No, none of that is unpleasant, or eerie either, as we first felt when coming up here. It all feels normal, or given, or handed down. Or maybe, in our case, just loaned for a while.

"Why just loaned?" Jay says. "We're making all this ours."

"We're only tourists."

"Not me. I'm a white settler."

It's a joke—or maybe it's not—that she and the Colonel have begun sharing at evening tea in front of the pine fire. He has christened her a white settler, which is a considerable step up from tourist class. The rest of us, the gentleman and his wife from Perth, the blushing red-haired doctor and her mother from Cheltenham, and myself, have not been promoted, judging from Jay and the Colonel's cozy, sometimes exclusive chats. Moreover, she is the only one who can persuade him to play his pipes. When his wife inquires if he will play, his response is something like, "The walls won't hear of it. The milk in your tea would curdle." When Jay asks him, he studies his cane for a moment, then calls for Mrs. Macbeth, the housekeeper, who is second in command after the Colonel's wife. "Fetch my small pipes," he tells her. "I'll see if they're tuned." The pipes arrive quickly, for beaming Mrs. Macbeth, all in white, loves to hear them, carries them like a baby, then finds the edge of a chair on the fringe of our group and perches there, fiddling her fingers.

The Colonel arranges the instrument in his kilted lap as if it were more than an instrument, as if it were something alive and old and faithful, and stiff with arthritis. "These pipes have been in my family over two hundred years," he says, speaking slowly. "Before that the Macrimmons held possession. I have read, and been told by others who read elsewhere, that the Macrimmons were the great players. But you can't know anything about their sound from words. I would like to hear the Macrimmons play with my own ears." He begins to inflate the goatskin bag, pulling in breath like a middle-distance runner, his chest expanding with the bag (I am surprised at how hard and serious the breathing is), his brown fingers, speckled with pink and black spots, feeling over the keys. One thumb, his right, is missing its tip.

Suddenly, without further prelude, he is playing. The music is not mad with shrieks but sweetly gay, suggesting a shy bride and groom at their wedding dance, taking their first plunge together in public. And though he plays with his eyes closed, it's there, at his eyes, where the music begins. I close my own eyes and climb in the brilliant sunlight to the top of Bioda Buidhe, and there, resting on an elbow, look east across the valley toward Staffin Bay. My shirt is off. Jay is napping beside me. The Old Man of Storr is south of us now, out of sight. From time to time a sheep or a lamb calls up from the valley. A steady breeze off the sea keeps the small black flies from settling on my notebook or on us. A gull, a white speck, circles around a plateau far below, round the greens and browns and under the blues of the sky that meet and mix in the sunlight falling on Jay's shoulders and back, and on the clipped grass around our sweaters spread out and pointing one arm toward a patch of delicate yellow primroses, another toward the brown pebbled droppings, like baked beans, lying in a mound beside my shoes. One of the droppings has broken open, exposing its packed tobacco-like innards. I bend close to it, expecting a distillation of these mountains, and smell nothing, the secret of their fruits and waters either kept by the sheep or taken back by the grass and air in a cycle I am not lucky enough to visit.

I don't know how many tunes the Colonel played, but he concluded with "The Skye Boat Song" and "Amazing Grace."

At one point near the end—for an interval of several seconds—I thought he was going to quit in mid-note, collapse, and open his eyes for the last time, for his full chest seemed as caught and still as the hawk's above the candelabra in the great hall. The doctor saw it, her jaw tensed. Jay saw it too—one of her hands flew from her lap, toward him, and gripped the arm of her chair. The scene, Jay and the Colonel frozen like that in profile, seemed a detail from a medieval tapestry. The Virgin Princess recognizes—what?—not Death, for the Colonel's face has none of Death's dark grimness; just the opposite, his color is ruddy, manly, heightened by the pine fire to a state of agelessness, and it speaks to a power and charm which the Princess is fearful of losing. Whatever she sees, it makes her appear very fragile and beautiful, and I am only a poor witness to it, a stranger here.

Then his chest and the tendons in his neck relaxed and he finished the song in perfect control, letting the last notes settle about the room like a child's sleep. We were moved, as much by the music and the Colonel's playing of it as by the tenuous fact, I think, that we were all still there, wherever we were. Finally we broke the stillness with our applause and he acknowledged it with a nod to each, but with a smile and his hand to Jay.

Under the wide sky on Ullinish Point, I am reminded of buzzards and coconut and of the yellow bubbly glow on my mother's brow as she bent to adjust the wrinkles in Bette Davis' old and angry face. I am reminded of the pigeon with the Halloween eye keeping her eggs warm in our eavestrough in Des Moines and of the rose petals floating on Jay's lap in Grayling—of her nightly walks with the Colonel and Mollie and Brittle

and Glen, and of the Sunday we crossed the Mackinac Bridge
for the first time in thirteen years and drove to Marquette to
scatter Jenny's ashes. I am reminded of the ashes Freddy and I
rubbed on our fingers so the crawlers wouldn't slip through,
of the carved ebony cobras the gentleman from Perth sent
down with his wife because they wouldn't let him sleep, and
of the maggots boiling in the lamb that Jay and I saw beside
the stream the day we climbed down from Bioda Buidhe with
the salt of our sunlit passion still fresh on our skins; of the snow
still clinging in small brown reserves to the edges of the Upper
Peninsula woods, and the air clean and sharp, and the feel of
spring let loose with room to breathe and doing just fine; and
of the ice along Lake Superior's shore sinking into sand and
rough turf, or slipping away from outcropped rock, or melting
in gray pools on granite shelves, and of the lake itself tippled
white and mammoth and blue and independent; and of the
oreboat suddenly appearing in the distance, a sluggish shape
red about the haunches, that I would have enjoyed flicking off
the water if I'd had the finger for it; and of my mother angrily
turning off the multiplied red and yellow bitter faces of Bette
Davis, saying to me, "Go, if you're going," of Freddy turning
from the door in his wheelchair, hurt, saying, "Take it easy," of
Jenny looking down from the upstairs window of our house in
Des Moines, her face a pink smear behind the overhanging
icicles, and of my brother's face webbed in shadows under his
son's basketball net, saying, "Yes, I'll tell the others"—I am
reminded of the road that led to the house we'd lived in our
last year in Marquette, and the woods behind it, the aspen and
oak and maples, and of the rise among these trees from which
we could see the lake and the silo; and of how that road had

changed, of how the meadows and fields beside it were now taken over by houses quickly built from the same practical plan and standing shoulder to shoulder as if in a line of sober defense against anyone who might be crazy enough to break from the road for the fields behind them.

We came to the place where the house—our house, built on the old creamery's foundation—should have been and wasn't. Nor the silo either. Nor anything we remembered. "Aspen Estates" said a sign in the yard and beyond it the contractor's trailer, and beyond that the yellow gravel trucks, the bulldozer, and beyond those the fresh red clay road leading into the woods and toward the rise where we had planned to take the ashes. We sat in Schooltz's Oldsmobile, and I began to watch us sitting there, a third party, a third pair of eyes. I saw Bill Rau reach to turn on the radio—imagined it—for something loud with electric frenzy and grim sweaty skin and the promise of a quick lay while the dog was away; but he did not turn on the radio, he sat there looking tired and a little stupid while his wife absently played with a button on her coat looking lost and worried. I didn't disturb them. I left them alone near the scene, forever changed, of their blooming young marriage, where the field mice had slipped in that fall and run above their heads, where their daughter was learning to stand up and walk, where all three of them had sat among the slender aspens, among summer's long grasses, on a rise from which mother and father could point to the lake and say to the baby, "See, honey? See the lake? Lake?"

I woke up on Ullinish Point smelling coconut and hearing a bird scream. The coconut odor came from the large hedge of yellow azaleas at the edge of the drop-off. I didn't know where the scream came from; probably from below, near the water, for I could see no birds—no big birds—above me or anywhere over the rolling grassland sloping inland. I sat for a moment beside the hedge of azaleas, waiting to fully wake up. Jay was still curled in the sheep's nest; in her white smock she looked like a shepherd girl or an angel in a school play, even with that glossy black helmet of hair and the wicked curl next to her ear. The sun shone on her cheek, and she seemed to be smiling.

Taking the wine left from our lunch I stepped carefully around the hedge and found a place to sit on the lip of the precipice. Straight down three hundred feet I saw gulls scattering like confetti over rocks and crashing surf but I saw no big screamers. The surf was part sea and part Loch Bracadale from the north and part Loch Harport from the south. Across the sea was the United States. I thought about going back, wondering where we would live when we did go back, and all I could picture was a place like Skye, like Ullinish Point, and sitting on the edge of it with a bottle of red wine between my legs and the salt breeze in my face.

I heard a distant sound like a motorcycle choking to stay alive, and then I saw a fishing boat small as a duck bobbing on the Loch Bracadale side. If we stayed on Skye I could practice and become a ghillie and take tourists out in my boat. Ghillie for a day—£6.00. When the ghillie also fishes the fee is £5.00. The boat on Loch Bracadale played with her engine, revving it, and I thought of Rush Miller who lived across from us in Des Moines. Rush would sit on his motorcycle, winter or summer, it didn't matter, and twist those grips for five, ten, sometimes fifteen minutes—just sit there in his garage across the street and rev and whine, rev and whine. Then if it was nice weather he'd take the cycle out in the yard and wash and polish it, down on his knees going over every shiny part like an afflicted priest who, if he only rubbed it long enough, could make that terribly precious thing breathe. Afterwards he'd stand back a ways and gaze a long time at it. And then he would fetch his camera and take its picture.

The fishing boat finally got her engine running smoothly and soon was a speck going over toward Macleod's Maidens across the loch. Yes, if we stayed on Skye I could fish near those maidens. And tend sheep near the Old Man of Storr and near all the other figure-like rocks on the island that were standing and waiting, gazing out to sea. Or sitting and waiting, like I was. But waiting for what? For the secret? Or only for dinner and evening tea? For Jay and the Colonel to pass arm in arm below our bedroom, and to hear him say he fell out of bed last night and lay on the floor for at least two hours, unable to get up?

"You must have been cold," Jay said.

"Yes. I was very cold."

"I wish I had been there to help you."

Maybe that was the secret. Falling out of bed in old age and having the Princess nearby to help you up again. I asked the gulls down below if that was a good guess, but they paid no attention. They had left the rocks and surf and were steadily rising, working at their weaving patterns. I watched them come up to my height and higher, soaring and dipping and veering close to my perch. I thought of the doves that flew past our window and of Jay waking me early one morning to see the buzzard attacking a young one, and the Colonel's wife that evening grimly announcing in a low voice they'd have to shoot the filthy things, to which the Colonel, not so deaf, responded,

"What's that woman mumbling about again? My buzzards? I thought all my murderous relatives were dead."

"So you can hear well enough, can you?" she said. "I'll tell the doctor not to come out, then. Much good *he* would have done." She turned to the rest of us. "It's the same with the pills my husband takes," she continued. "Totally worthless, they are. He eats every kind and color he finds lying around—his own, the dogs', and even Mrs. Macbeth's when he stumbles across them. Perhaps one night I'll murder him—in a fit of passion, of course—and be done with it. All that nonsense about the pill-taking, I mean. Extraordinary how they've got us bamboozled. You don't bamboozle your patients, I trust?" she asked the blushing doctor from Cheltenham, adding quickly, "Don't answer that, my dear. I'm off on what my husband calls 'a stump' or 'a cricket,' I can't remember which. Perhaps it's neither. In any case, when his hearing finally does go, that'll finish the playing, I suppose. A pity. I've always loved his playing."

At this last remark, delivered with an uncustomary lack of thrust and charge, she seemed suddenly embarrassed, as though she'd confessed a feeling, an intimacy, she had rather kept to herself. And further, completely out of character, she seemed at a loss as to how to go on from there. She was also, I realized, trying to avoid looking at Jay sitting beside the Colonel, and not succeeding. It was a crack in a rock-like commanding presence I had not thought possible. But there it was, for she finally said, in a tone that was unmistakable, "Of course for the present he'll still play the small pipes, at least when you ask him, won't he, Mrs. Rau?" Without waiting for a response, she used her cane to stand up. "Well," she sighed wearily, an old woman who must attend to her paying guests, "we're all having tea, aren't we, so I'd better see if Mrs. Macbeth needs a hand."

When I stood up behind the hedge of azaleas to see if Jay was awake yet, she was gone. Our picnic things were gone too. I stepped around the hedge and began to look for her along the rim of the Point, where she might have found a perch like mine. But she wasn't anywhere along the rim, and on the rolling grassland sloping inland toward the causeway I saw only the small flock of sheep grazing. She must have returned to the car, I thought. I started back, following close to the Loch Harport side of the Point, the fastest route. The causeway was half an hour's walk; the car, parked on the bluff above it, another fifteen minutes. Straight up in the sky, a lark was riding the stiff late afternoon breeze and blowing its head off.

I called out Jay's name. Called again. But all I heard was the lark, who seemed to be drifting back with me, singing louder and faster. I had to be careful of the drop-off, for I was only a few feet from the edge, and jogging now. Over the edge I could see where Loch Harport changed from dark blue to light green to surf along the rocky shoreline. The white surf looked very tame from where I was—everything looked tame, or placed there, constructed out of pretty clays and paints by a romantic giant child, including the rugged almond-colored Cuillin Hills rising into the clouds beyond the loch—and the lark's job was to keep me awake to enjoy it. Then I spotted her. She was near the water, about ten inches tall, standing among a pile of boulders. Moving as close to the edge as I dared, I called out and waved. She waved back.

Hugging the cliff in a grassy, rocky, narrow zig-zag was the only path she could have taken down there. I took it, stepping carefully, passing clusters of primroses and sheep turds. As I got near the bottom, she started climbing over the boulders away from me.

The boulders lay a hundred and fifty yards along the foot of the cliff wall, crashed against in places by the loch. Her glossy black helmet disappeared among them. Moments later she reappeared, at the peak of a pile of boulders thirty yards away, casually swinging the picnic basket. She turned, facing me, the wind furling her smock smoothly around her legs and breasts. She gave me a big grin, then quickly slid down the other side out of sight again.

By the time I got to that same peak, she had slipped around somehow, and now was back where I had been, inching down a flat sloping boulder on her seat toward the loch crashing in. I waited to see how far she would go; the water was no warmer than fifty degrees—and the air cool and getting cooler down here in the shadows beside the cliff wall—and if she slid off the boulder she'd be in up to her neck. She stopped, and slowly pulled the smock to her hips, letting the spray fall on her bare legs. Then she turned her face toward me, cheek on shoulder, in the mock pose of a fetching wide-eyed starlet. Straight up the cliff behind her, the sun was about to slip past the hedge of azaleas, but before it did here was a shot in color for the *Skye Tourist Guide*.

Leaving my peak I started in her direction. I had to go around an enormous boulder that blocked my view of her, and when I got around it she'd gone again. Thirsty, and tired of carrying the wine bottle, I finished off the last couple of swallows and wedged the bottle between two rocks. I was also sweating. Up and down she bobbed, grinning, posing, mocking nearly every modeling posture in the book—the naughty, sexy, innocent, wind-swept, cutely flustered—like the poses in the album she kept in Detroit when I met her—and I following, picking up the picnic basket, her sneakers, her underpants, and neither of us saying anything, not even when we were close enough to reach out over the gulf between two boulders and touch hands. Which we didn't do either.

Finally, at the foot of the zig-zagging path hugging the cliff wall, on a grassy shelf, she sat still. I came and sat beside her. We said nothing for a few minutes, just sat there catching our breath.

"I saw something floating on the water," she said at last. "I thought it was your cap."

"When?"

"When I woke up from my nap and didn't see you."

"Why didn't you yell out before coming down here? I was just behind the azaleas."

"I don't know. Maybe I did, a little."

"Are you all right?"

"I'm fine. It was good exercise, all that"—she waved toward the boulders, swallowing hard—"nonsense. God, I'm thirsty!"

"You banged your knee."

"It's nothing. I bruise easily, remember?"

"It's bleeding."

"So what?"

"Here, wipe it off with this napkin."

"Did you like my—performance?"

"It was quite a show. You're in good shape."

"Good shape. Jesus. Is that all you care about?"

"No."

"Well, tell me, Bill. Did you get any good ideas, watching? What did I remind you of?"

"You. Your old modeling pictures."

"My modeling pictures? That's all?"

"Yes."

She lay back her head and closed her eyes. "I wish I had something to drink," she said.

I found a few grapes in the basket and gave them to her. We looked at the sea.

She said, suddenly, bitterly, "Inspiration. The magic moment. I was doing it before I knew I was doing it. Strictly unplanned. The panties bit, though, now that was housecleaning first, and whatever else second. I'd got some dirt in them taking a slide on this path. Some path, wouldn't you say?"

"Want them back?" I took the underpants out of the basket.

"Sure. I'm getting cold down there. Maybe I should say colder."

"What is it, Jay?"

"Everything. Me, you. You know that."

"We're doing the best we can."

"Oh, I suppose we are. We eat and sleep, we walk out here and eat and nap and bound around on the boulders. We climb in the Quiraing and eat and nap and—oh Billy, I'm so tired of it!"

"We can leave Skye if you've had enough."

"That's not what I'm talking about. Please, Billy."

"Put your pants on."

"We haven't been close in months."

"You've been taken care of."

"Damn you. Damn you, Billy."

"I've been taken care of, too."

"Please, please—help me. What can I *do?*"

"I don't know."

"What are *you* doing? Tell me."

"You can think about things."

Her hands came together, trembling.

"I didn't mean to say that, Jay. I really didn't. I'm sorry."

"I loved her as much as you did."

"I know you did."

She stood then, and swung around to face me, as if to say more, explain something; but she said nothing, instead thrust her fists to her temples, knuckling at them in an upward motion, as if something had lodged in the pores of her skin and was hurting her—and moaning, her face wrinkled and turned a sickly white, like a mean, ghostly caricature of a face in false mourning, except that there wasn't anything false about Jay's grief, and I knew it.

Yet a part of me had stepped aside and was auditing the scene, a dispassionate, clinical, academic, bloodless part of me, and it wanted the rest of me to simply observe that this wrinkled, white-faced caricature was the real thing. That the actress who had earlier demonstrated her ability to mock various modeling postures was now putting on a show of grief and loss and confusion and fear. Observe her and appreciate her talent and fix in your mind the details of her performance if you think they are worth saving, the Auditor said, but remember, it's only a performance like all the others—the Detroit performance, the Upper Peninsula, the Iowa, the Wedding, the Miscarriages, the Dancing on the Elm Stump, the Picnics on

Lake Superior, the Storybook House, the Child, the Muse, the Flight with the Urn to the Hartwick Pines, all of them, including the Father O'Donnel, the Colonel, the Almost Ph.D.—and me too, the Auditor said, I had been performing with her, I was part of the act, making my own faces, my own speeches— the Suitor's, the Poet's, the Father's, the Betrayed Husband's, the Lover's—and believing in them as much as she had believed in hers. We were a good match, not made in Heaven, by any means, nor on plain dirt, either, but somewhere in between— in the corners and pockets of our own vain and blood-thick curlicued brains. And for a total of seventy-six years, her thirty-six and my forty, we had been practicing for this picture-book dramatic moment of grief on the boulders near the edge of a loch on the Isle of Skye with nothing around to distract us but a few crying gulls and a crazy lark. It was simply another dramatic moment—in a setting rich and romantic, fit for the card shops. We could add it to our repertoire. Then we could continue, carry on. Maybe in the carrying-on, just maybe, we would find some originality, if we were lucky—but that was doubtful, because we knew too much.

That's what the part of me that had stepped aside to audit the scene had decided, or had offered for me to think in a corner of my head, and I began to shiver, knowing it was not true, that it was evil and cynical, and I looked at her face which appeared almost phosphorescent now, smoothed out, sugar bowl–smooth under the black helmet, and at her eyes which were all burnt-brown and shiny and still and hard, like a doll's, and leveled at my own but unseeing, as if I were not there or she were blind, and the shivering increased. A squeezing ache attacked my chest, it held on tight, tighter, and then suddenly it let go, and in its place there was nothing, just an absence of ache, a hole where the ache had been—and for an instant I thought *it is true, all of it, we're as good as dead,* and then the sugar bowl–smooth skin on her face wrinkled again, slowly, as if a time mechanism had been tripped, and then her eyes saw me, a monster, an emptiness, and she screamed and turned and started over the boulders toward the loch. I caught her near the edge and held her. I held her for a long time, hard, and then she began to hold me. We pressed our faces against each other's necks until the gulls had all come down from their circling and were settled on the rocks, and the sun had settled, and the lark gone home. Everything was quiet except the waves and the wind. I picked up the picnic basket and we walked back to the car.

*

There are at least nineteen hours of daylight on the island now, maybe more, for it is not really dark when we go to bed around midnight and fully bright when we wake at six. Mrs. Macbeth told me it was light until three o'clock yesterday morning; she'd heard Mollie carrying on in the Colonel's room, and went in to find him on the floor again. She is very worried about him. I told her I would not be going out to Dunvegan Head anymore and canceled the lunch she'd been packing for me. If I write in my journal now I write mainly in our room, after evening tea, when Jay is out strolling with the Colonel and his dogs. Combing her hair before going down-stairs tonight, she said, "He has a croft in the Trotternish. He said I could live there." I watched her looking off at the almost white sky, combing her hair with slow, thoughtful strokes, the hair shiny and black and moving under her comb like a muscular skin. A seal named Hoover lives in the New England Aquarium. In the early hours when drunks come to bathe in his pool, Hoover greets them by saying, "Hello, dare," and then his name. I said to Jay, "I'm thinking about Hoover, the seal." She continued to comb her hair. After a while she stood up. "He said I could have Brittle and Glen for companionship."

The Colonel and Jay walk below our window and over the lawn, past the dovecote, to the edge of the pines. Arm in arm they walk, very slowly, almost stiffly, as if practicing for a formal pageant. There should be harpsichord music in the background. Usually the Colonel will point up in the trees with his cane—probably directing Jay's eye to the buzzards' nest. Then they follow along the fringe of the pines to the garden in front of the house, where they stand facing the sea and the first star. They are much less stiff standing there, and would make a good etching for an old-fashioned book—a romance by Scott—or a good picture for the stereopticon. Mollie is always beside them, looking more like a sheep than a dog. Brittle and Glen wander about. Sometimes Jay finds a stick and throws it for them to fetch. She calls them "the boys." The other guests, I've noticed, are calling them "the boys" now, too.

The gentleman from Perth and his wife said good-bye this morning, which I think pleased the Colonel's wife; twice this week when we exchanged brief pleasantries with her in the great hall, she poked her cane at the carved ebony cobras coiling on the table beside the parakeets, and declared, "They simply don't *belong* down here." Maybe because the cobras were never alive and only real animals, stuffed or otherwise, may occupy the hall; or maybe she just likes things where she puts them, skittish gentlemen from Perth or no. Or maybe—it occurs to me now—the key word is "belong" and she is really hinting that *we've* been in her house long enough. I would bet on the last with more confidence than when I posted my three pounds on Troy in the Derby—a horse I knew nothing about except that its name is linked with a great illiterate and probably blind poet.

In 1899 a Gurkha warrior named Thapa went up Glamaig Mountain in his bare feet in thirty-seven minutes and descended in eighteen. At the top he paused only long enough to turn around. Half a century later one George Rhodes, attempting to beat Thapa's time, went up in thirty-seven and a half minutes and came down in nineteen, wearing basketball shoes. A man named Captain Maryon left Sligachan one day for a walk and never returned. His skeleton was found eighteen months later on this remote rocky slope of Sgurr na Strigh, where I'm sitting now. A friend of Captain Maryon built a nine-foot-high stone cairn to mark the spot. The cairn is in the shape of a perfect pyramid. It rises from a base of dark heavy chunks of gabbro to stones, at the peak, the size of a baby's fist. It is hard to guess how long it took the man to build this monument. Perhaps as long as it took a settler on the prairie to bust the sod, sow his seed, and harvest the crop. Perhaps longer. Perhaps—if you count everything—as long as it takes a man to build his woman a house.

From Sligachan it took me four hours to climb and descend Glamaig, and at least three hours more, judging by the sun, to reach Captain Maryon's monument. It took Troy two minutes and thirty-seven seconds to win the English Derby, earning me eighteen pounds, or just about thirty-seven dollars at the current rate of exchange. I see that I'm building a small body of figures in which the number thirty-seven stands out. Jay will be thirty-seven next year. My sister Helen is thirty-seven now. The numbers on the house that my father built for my mother are the same. I think I could play this game until the almond-colored sky turns dark, and in the end all I'd have is another list. I'm tired of making lists. Nevertheless it is true that I counted my steps back from the point on the Au Sable where we figured the doe had jumped last summer, and where we finally emptied the urn, so that if we ever wanted to return, we could start at the second bridge and count off thirty-seven paces and be there.